G000054887

A Moment in Time

A Moment in Time

JEFF MORRIS

RESOURCE *Publications* · Eugene, Oregon

A MOMENT IN TIME

Copyright © 2018 Jeff Morris. All rights reserved. Except for brief quotations in critical publications or reviews, no part of this book may be reproduced in any manner without prior written permission from the publisher. Write: Permissions, Wipf and Stock Publishers, 199 W. 8th Ave., Suite 3, Eugene, OR 97401.

Resource Publications
An Imprint of Wipf and Stock Publishers
199 W. 8th Ave., Suite 3
Eugene, OR 97401

www.wipfandstock.com

PAPERBACK ISBN: 978-1-5326-6207-2
HARDCOVER ISBN: 978-1-5326-6208-9
EBOOK ISBN: 978-1-5326-6209-6

Manufactured in the U.S.A.   10/05/18

To my mom and dad, for demonstrating the way of love.

Preface

IT'S OFTEN TRUE THAT we only appreciate a thing when it's contrasted with its opposite. I can offer a few examples to illustrate the point. Spring temperatures are most coveted just after a long cold winter, but even after just a few weeks, we begin to hear complaints about the heat. The same is true in terms of our health. I normally don't give much thought to the fact that I'm in good health—blessed with the ability to do physical labor or even climb a mountain, if I felt so inclined—until I fall ill with the flu. It's only after a few days of being incapacitated that I feel an overwhelming sense of relief when I return to my "normal" state, which, in retrospect, is an appreciation I should carry nearly all the time. We find an even more accessible example in being hungry or thirsty. I'm sure everyone has experienced a moment of extreme thirst, when a simple cup of water seemed as though it were a miracle from heaven, because it was a moment when the contrast between being really thirsty, and not thirsty at all, was most wide.

It's in this context that our main character finds himself, as I believe we all often do, without necessarily realizing it. We're all confronted with a stark contrast in how we could perceive reality. On the one hand, we could understand existence as a matter of random chance—meaningless—and on such a view we are forced to relinquish things such as rationality, love, morality, gratitude, and even beauty. On the other hand, if we believe that life is objectively meaningful, the whole thing turns on its head. We believe we will find order in nature, that logic is possible, that murder really is wrong, and that beautiful pieces of art or the gentle touch from our beloved are worthy of gratitude. I don't think many people would question the merit in accepting the second option as the more palpable one, but the problem we encounter is that meaning can only be had if we accept that God is the one who created us—a situation our pride, and secular culture, has something to comment on, even for all of its benefits.

In all of these contrasts, there's also a third way of perceiving reality, and it's one that we simple creatures fall into all too easily. This would be to take a position of apathy and walk through the middle, so to speak. On this view, one doesn't understand that life, or our actions, are meaningful, but neither does one attempt to fully live out (as though it were logically possible) a meaningless existence. It's here that we often find ourselves, both the religious and non-religious, paralyzed in a sort of existential purgatory. It's an easy trap to fall into because although the seasons change, and the sun comes up new every morning, we end up doing our daily business with a sense of ordinariness, as though flowers and chipmunks are "normal." It's here that we no longer contemplate the majesty of the great oak tree, or stand in awe of a ravishing thunderstorm. This state of indifference is one which, for obvious reasons, all of us should encourage each other to avoid. For what if the mechanic just didn't feel like tightening your lug nuts, or the engineer didn't find it necessary to measure for the right load-bearing joists, or the doctor didn't really care if he killed all the cancer cells, or the father didn't try to love his children even after they disappointed him? I believe it's unavoidable that any sort of relativist or postmodern view will lead to precisely this kind of passive attitude, and that we should, at all costs, religious or not, try to prevent it. It might have been avant-garde to conjure these modern ideas, but it's a real drag to live them out.

According to the Bible, it makes perfect sense that our attitudes toward life would often fall into one of these three camps. It says that God made people in order to be in a loving relationship with them, and therefore we have an intrinsic sense of longing to be with him. The problem is that Adam sinned, as we all often do—the ramification of creating creatures that know they exist, we just can't get over ourselves—and we currently reside in a place where we don't quite belong. To me this account of the world makes the most sense to explain things like suffering, evil, guilt, where we came from, beauty, courage, love, and why so many of us experience a real relationship with God. If there was no God, there would be no such thing as love, or even suffering. It also leads us down three often intersecting roads: (1) We hold close to God and trust that we will be with him some day without the interruption of sin. (2) We curse God for our own selfishness, even denying his existence. Or, (3) we generally coast along and find our meaning in simple pleasures or work, wishing for the whole experience to be over very soon, or at the very least, without any more suffering. Of course, the first road is where Christians generally want to travel, but even believers find themselves on the other two roads more often than we would like to admit. Thank our heavenly father for forgiveness.

If you're not a Christian, then after reading the story you might have questions regarding the truth of Christianity. You might wonder why you should choose Christianity over other religions, or why you can't be a rational naturalist, or how we know that God isn't evil rather than good and loving, and I encourage you to continue on your quest for answers. You'll come across many opinions against the claims about God, his son, and his spirit, but with a little bit of tact, you'll be able to see that anger and deceit often cloud the arguments against him. Don't forget your Bible stories. Jesus spent his time healing the poor, sick, and lonely, and they crucified him for it. You may also be tempted to judge the whole thing based on the reputation of Christians you know, or the crusades, or some other atrocity done in the name of Christianity, but this would be a mistake. The only reputation that matters is that of Jesus Christ, the historic man who the entire world developed their calendar around, and whose birth we celebrate at Christmas, because he is the only perfect example of how a Christian ought to be. I've never in all my life heard of a case when someone sought to understand God with a genuine heart and didn't find Him.

For certain parts of the book I've set aside my personal views to explore the contrast to them. I found the task interesting for the most part, but also tedious at times. On a few occasions I wanted to wring a certain character's neck, but since I know the stubbornness of my own heart, I developed a sort of patience with the man.

It's also worth noting that I make no doctrinal claims, other than what's generally agreed upon by Christians around the world. Any appearance of being denomination-specific is just that—an appearance.

Jeff Morris

Acknowledgements

THANK YOU, TIM, FOR diving with me endlessly into the bit of things. And thank you, Lisa, for taking on the challenge of editing such a work as this.

1

IT WAS A NORMAL morning by all accounts, and a busy one at that. After waking up I had done my usual routine.

First I went around the apartment to make sure the drapes remained sealed across each window. Over time the adhesive from the tape that I had used to secure them tightly to the wall would become worn and lose its gluey quality. I couldn't be sure when the adhesive would fail, and it wasn't worth the risk to just wait and see. In the past, I had waited for the tape to come undone before securing a new piece. But after having spent so much time protecting myself from the outside world, only to be infiltrated because the sticky substance on a small piece of tape had failed, wasn't worth the risk or the anxiety.

The rest of my routine involves a series of calculated steps that I had carefully developed since moving into the building. There's squishing the trash in the trash basket to make room for more, or if the trash can't be squished any further, shuffling the bag to a new spot under the sink and starting a new one. I've worked out a system whereby I only need to take my trash out two, maybe three times per year. This of course saves energy, but more importantly, reduces the risk of me coming into contact with what's out there.

The next item on the list is breakfast, and once I'm finished eating, I normally have to shuffle around the dishes in the sink. Over the course of several days I'll end up using various sizes of plates, bowls, cups, and utensils. In order to eliminate the number of times that I have to wash the dishes, and prevent the shrill clang of handling porcelain, which could draw unnecessary attention to my abode, I let them sit in the sink until I can't fit any more. What I don't think other people realize is that if you stack similarly shaped dishes together, with the large plates at the bottom, followed by the small plates, and then the bowls, you can substantially increase the sink space, and hold off on washing dishes for up to a week. The task is straight forward, and only takes simply organizing skills to accomplish, but translates into a huge payoff for the efforts. I sometimes take this concept even further by using disposable dishes, which can push my dish washing timeline out two, sometimes even three weeks. Unfortunately, this method ruffles with my trash plan and I've yet to find the right balance.

Once these tasks are complete, I tend to focus on one of the many projects I've started around the apartment. It takes my mind off things when I'm keeping busy. Today, I planned to paint the walls in my living room again. They're currently dark gray, and they get slightly darker with each new coat of paint. I would have gone with my instincts and painted the walls black, but since the trim, drapes, kitchen cupboards, and most of the furniture is black, I thought the contrast would be more visually appealing. I often wonder if I made the right decision.

I began readying my paint supplies, taking the brushes and paint cans from under the sink, preparing myself for another long day. It's worth pointing out here that something strange happens to a man's senses when he's been in quiet solitude as long as I have. I might be getting up there in age, but not so much that I can blame physical incapacities on the passage of time. It was being alone that altered my state. This is so much the case that the slightest sound seems to reverberate, making my eardrums pound as though a marching band were playing in my skull. So, with my body half buried under the kitchen sink while I rummaged around looking for some rags, and my mind consumed by the color dark gray, my ears suddenly burned with intensity, as though several wasps had flown in and attacked when I heard the creak of the mail slot opening. I turned quickly to look at the front door of my apartment and watched a small black envelop slip through the open crack and land on the floor.

I closed the cupboard door and stepped toward the letter, trying to be as quiet as I could. I had heard the mail man leave, but something told me to be careful about the amount of noise I was making. I picked up the letter from the floor and when I saw that the return address was the same address as my own, I knew who the letter had come from. Without hesitation I ripped open the outside flap and pulled the paper from its cocoon.

Dear John,

You've been our tenant for some time, and we're glad that you're living here. We value all of our residents, and want you to make the most of your stay. We notice that you don't go out of your apartment much to enjoy the building or the property. If you have read the other letters, you'll remember that you have unlimited access to all of the amenities. We first wrote to you because we thought you might have forgotten this. We were hopeful that a friendly reminder would stir your memory.

When we noticed that you ignored the first letter, we wrote a second one. This time we sensed that you had become scared of us. This is not uncommon. Our letters get ignored sometimes and we had explained when we wrote the second time that we had not taken it personally. When you didn't respond to the second letter, we became concerned, and wrote again. In the third letter, you'll remember that we described the facility and amenities of the property in great detail. We find that when people stop using the amenities, they forget what the building and the property has to offer. In your case these letters have thus far proved ineffective.

There's one more item to cover and then I have a request. I'm sure you haven't forgotten, but your building will be torn down very soon. All of our residents have been informed. Do you remember the sign that's hanging from the door of your apartment, or the ones near the entrance to the building? Sometimes people ignore the signs and that's when we start sending letters. If you need a reminder, here's what they say:

"Please use the amenities as much as possible."

"Your building will be torn down. Please become familiar with the road to the new building."

We're afraid that you won't know the way to the new
building, or worse yet, that you won't want to leave this
one when it gets torn down.

We want to meet face to face. If you're not using the
amenities, or listening to the signs, there must be a good
reason, and we would like to know what that reason is.

At your convenience, please come down to the basement.
I'm always there, day and night.

Sincerely,

Sam

Assistant to the Headmaster

I could remember getting the other letters. I could also remember throwing them in the trash shortly after I'd read them.
I put this one down and took a moment to consider my options.

For a number of years, the group that was now sending me
letters seemed to be targeting me. Then, for a long while they had
left me mostly to myself, only promoting their message passively
through signs hanging around the building. It seemed their tactics
were again becoming aggressive. I can remember this one time,
just after I first moved into the building, a man wearing a janitorial
uniform came up to me in the lobby. It was the first encounter.

I had been working as a professor of science and lost my position due matters beyond my control. I won't get into the details,
but you know how professors can be—even deans—when faced
with intellectual superiority. With my pension lost, I decided to
get a smaller place. While I was carrying my burden of despair,
this man walked right up and shook my hand. The encounter was
startling, as I was quite vulnerable at the time, and with no other
companions, I welcomed the sudden camaraderie.

It didn't take long for the interaction to sour. After working
through some niceties, he suddenly began spouting all kinds of
nonsense about some sort of terrorist group or cult. I listened
politely at first; being new to the building, I didn't want to make

any enemies. He capitalized on my attention, and before long had explained the intricacies of how the world would end in fire, and that judgement was coming, and that it was the aim of his group to take over not just the building, or the city, but the entire world. I wouldn't have been quite so alarmed if not for the sheer self-confidence of the man—his unwavering belief was frightening.

When he noticed my attention beginning to wane, he began talking about the building, with which he was completely enamored. He spoke about some amenities, and a road near the building. Then, he asked about my apartment, how long I planned to live there, and even seemed to suggest that I shouldn't get too comfortable, because I wouldn't be here for long. It was all very eccentric, and intrusive.

Before long, matters became nearly unbearable. I started having similar experiences with other men, some dressed in uniforms and some not, for the following few months—and not just around the building. I began running into them at the grocery store, the hardware store, and even public washrooms. It wasn't just that I was being followed. The group began employing passive tactics specifically designed to brainwash people by displaying relentless propaganda messages. I had read about situations like these in stories, but never thought it could happen to me. That's when I began taking precautions. I didn't have the wherewithal to move and couldn't be sure if I could get away from them if I did. Since then, I hadn't heard from them directly. Years had passed without so much as a glimpse of the uniformed men, until a few months ago when they started sending me letters.

I felt nervous because of this new interaction, but their relentlessness was telling, and caused a major disruption to my routine.

In a sudden moment of boldness, provoked by their intrusion, I decided that the only solution was to oblige their request and finally confront them directly.

2

I PUT AWAY THE paint brush and began my search for clothing. I knew that if I was going to be out for a while, I needed to take the necessary precautions for protecting myself from the environment. For as long as I could remember, the air had been thick with pollution, but since moving to the building, I had the suspicion that someone had released some sort of contaminants into the air inside the building. My body had reached near decrepitude since moving in, with the soreness of my muscles and the headaches getting progressively worse every year. I had also determined that although the air was thick outside the building, it didn't have the wretched stench that lingered inside, further confirming my suspicion.

Not allowing the unseemly atmosphere to seep into my sanctuary is one of the reasons I had fixed my blinds to the walls in my apartment; aside from not wanting to see my neighbors. I had found that the same dingy glaze that hovered in the hallways had made its way through my windows and into my living space. I hadn't yet found a way to get the air out, but with the tape, had found that I could stop more from coming in. I wasn't sure how other people had learned to live with the air, but they must have their own systems for keeping it out, similar to mine—unless they had simply accepted their fate.

As I finished putting on my second pair of socks, I considered what their motives might be for wanting a face-to-face meeting about the condition of the building. The likely answer was that they wanted to understand how their brainwashing tactics were affecting the residents' psyche, so they could decide if alterations were necessary. It came to me just then that maybe the letter writer, Sam, wanted me out of my apartment. He'll get me to concede to its deplorable condition, and then explain how there are better apartments in the building, moving me to a more vulnerable location. Or maybe he had snuck in when I was out picking up paint and had seen the progress I had made to the habitat. Once I vacate, he'll take it for himself. It's only a matter of time before a group like them starts taking whatever they want.

As I finished putting on my second t-shirt, I made up my mind to stand firm. No matter how appealing he made it sound, I wasn't going to give up my apartment. I had spent years trying to make the best of things and I wasn't about to start over because of intimidation. I finished my ritual by putting on my jacket, hat, scarf, and gloves.

I stepped outside the apartment and locked the door behind me. I hadn't been out for a long time and the air unexpectedly seemed to get slightly better as soon as I stepped into the hallway. I walked down the long corridor toward the elevator and all along the way I kept my head down and my hands buried deep into my pockets, wishing to be invisible. When I reached the end of the hall, I carefully inspected the elevator before pushing the down button. As I waited for the doors to open, I looked back down the hall and saw two of my neighbors, a married couple, walk out of their apartment. I pushed the down button several times to try and speed up the process, but the doors weren't opening fast enough.

Aside from the dingy air and the forced isolation, the worst part about the building was the other people. After my first encounter with the cult, I realized that most of the residents were part of the same group, and just as forthright in their intent to convince me to join them. Whenever I ran into someone in the hall or out on the street, they would ask me questions that weren't particularly useful, other than to pinpoint my weaknesses. They often spoke about a road that would lead to a utopia that was ruled by a man called the Headmaster. The Headmaster seemed to be a fictitious Machiavellian caricature, used by the group to convey the idea that they were a consolidated bunch. No one had ever seen the man—every one of them would admit to this much.

The more I conversed with the people around the building, the more I began to suspect that I might be the only one who was still resisting our conundrum. I wasn't sure if the average IQ of the common resident was dropping, but I could tell from the way they spoke with such naivety that it was highly likely. I also didn't understand why everyone, other than myself, was so cheery all the time. Had they any inkling of their surroundings? If they weren't going to think for themselves, they should at least recognize their imprisonment and not be so thrilled by it.

At first I would plan every time that I needed to leave the apartment in such a way that I wouldn't mistakenly run into someone, so I could avoid subjecting myself to their meaningless ramblings. I suspected that if I exposed my mind to their chitchat too many times, I might not be able to hold my sanity indefinitely and may begin doing as they did. I'd spent considerable energy on the matter, even waking up early to determine their patterns. My research told me that most people were in the halls of the building between eight and nine in the morning. There was also a better chance of running into them in the late afternoon and early evening. Times could vary extensively when outside the building, making it much more unpredictable to go outdoors. My solution was to buy things in bulk such as groceries, project suppliers, and basic living necessities. I stocked up on the essentials and had learned to cope without the luxuries by only getting them when I had to pick up the essentials. The system worked well and continuing to improve it had been a priority.

"Hi John, it's nice to see you out today," said my neighbor, who stood smiling with his wife.

I could sense the tension in their eyes, but couldn't decide what they wanted, or why they were speaking in such a nice tone.

"You're bundled up. Is it supposed to be cold today?" he continued cheerfully.

He then turned to his wife and remarked, "Maybe we need more layers."

The elevator chimed, indicating that this conversation was about to get squished into a tiny inescapable space. The doors opened and one of my other neighbors walked out of the small steel box.

"Oh, hi Ben, we've been meaning to speak with you about dinner," the man who came out of the elevator said to my neighbor.

I slipped past the group, and as the three of them huddled in the hallway, I pushed the close door button inside the elevator several times. The doors slowly shut, but not before the man peaked his eyes between the diminishing crack and smiled. I felt a sense of relief and pushed the B button. It was a close call.

As the elevator made its descent toward the basement, I used the time to compile my thoughts. I ordered my priorities in such a way that I would only speak on topics related to the improvement of the building, but if I could, I would also try to gain an understanding of what the group was really after. I had to be careful and not allow Sam to somehow manipulate me. The elevator started to slow, and when it stopped, the chime indicated that I had arrived at the basement.

I had never been to the basement of the building. When the doors opened, I was surprised to find that the dingy air had lightened even more. I was cautious at first, and wanted to make sure I understood my surroundings before committing myself. I walked carefully out of the doors and into a large room with light gray walls. The ceiling seemed so tall that when I looked up, I felt dizzy and lost. I could make out row upon row of large chandeliers lining the ceiling through the hazy fog of the dingy air, and then realized that they had used them to make the basement seem a little less dingy and a little less dark than the rest of the building. The floor was made of marble and stretched as far as my eyes could see. When I looked closely at it, I could see intricate swirls of gray and dark gray. Other than the grandeur of the room, and the large chandeliers, there was nothing out of the ordinary to observe.

In the center of the room, far from where I was standing, I could see a desk with a man sitting at it. I paused for a moment, squinting my eyes relentlessly, somehow thinking the act would help me formulate my first impression of the man. I walked slowly toward the center of the room, careful not to take my eyes too far away from the lonely silhouette. I thought to myself that if this man was trying to swindle me, he had picked the wrong guy to tangle with. My nerves felt sharp and I readied myself for confrontation. The echo of my feet bounced off the walls as I made my approach to the desk.

"John, we're so glad that you came right away. I'm Sam. Come, have a seat."

He stood before he made his greeting and had announced it as if he was introducing a boxer into the ring. His voice clanged throughout the large space and filled the basement auditorium with a brief sense of warmth. I felt insecure at his delighted greeting and wanted to cower away, or run back toward the elevator.

For some reason, I couldn't help but to concede to his request and slid my way into the wooden chair. It had a straight back and was very solid. The design forced me to sit with almost perfect posture, with my back as straight as a board. The sensation was both painful and irresistible.

His desk was wide and a small stack of blank papers and black envelopes lay on the corner closest to me. There was one pen resting in the middle of the desk, and a piece of folded paper sat in front of him. When we made eye contact across the large wooden barrier, it felt like Sam was sitting right on top of me, and I looked away quickly. His smile was beaming and his eyes were open wide. I wondered if I was the first person to respond to one of his letters. It looked to me like he had a system and that he was glad that someone had finally taken his bait. I had learned over the years to never speak first when someone wants something from you, or when you want something from someone else, so we sat in silence while he stared at me.

"Would you like some tea?" he asked. "I was about to take a break and have one myself. Now that you're here, we can have one together."

I was a bit startled by the question. The offer of tea was the last thing I had expected him to say, unless he was preparing to play the long game with me.

"No, I'm fine," I said, before quickly looking toward the ground.

The second thing I had learned about negotiating was to pretend that you're not at all interested in the situation. Giving the impressions that nothing about the encounter matters, and it is all just a waste of time, should get the other person to cut to the chase and show their true intentions more quickly.

"I bet you haven't had a tea like this one. Try some—it satisfies from the first sip to the last gulp," he cajoled.

I looked up from the ground and saw a cup of tea steaming at the edge of the desk right in front of me. Sam clenched his cup with both hands and took the aroma slowly into his nose as he squinted his eyes and curled his shoulders toward each other. When I realized there was no kettle in the room, or stove, or anything other than Sam, his desk, and some papers, my whole body shook uncontrollably. I hoped that Sam hadn't noticed. It was obviously a well-orchestrated stunt, meant to shock me into vulnerability. Somehow I was able to remain calm and keep my composure, all the while wondering how he had produced the tea from thin air.

"How was the ride down?" he asked.

He's going to butter me up for awhile, I thought.

"It was fine," I said.

"Was it exciting to leave your apartment?"

"Exciting? More like dangerous."

"Oh?" said Sam, with a sense of curiosity in his tone.

"The air down here isn't so bad, but you should try living on the fifth floor where I am," I continued, without even thinking to hold my tongue.

Sam looked confused.

"Either you've never been outside of this basement, or you're trying to make me look foolish. Your letter said you wanted me down here to discuss the condition of the building, well, the polluted air is a good place to start." I said without a crack in my voice, reminding myself to stay calm, assertive, and stick to the topic of the building.

"Oh no, I don't live in the basement," he said with a light chuckle. "I was told to move my office down here. I used to have it on the top floor, and before that I worked outside."

"Sounds like you've be demoted," I snickered.

"Demoted?" asked Sam. "Why would you think that?"

It seemed he wanted to dance around for a while. I felt sure about my position of unwavering invulnerability, and my ability to hold it, so I decided to play along and follow his lead. My first impression of Sam's role was that the cult probably expected him to advance their strategies, but that he wasn't all that important. His clothes looked far too worn for someone who held a high position, and he had obviously just been demoted.

"At my job, when people went from the top floor to the basement, there was no other explanation." I felt good about the witty comment and wanted to keep Sam on his heels.

"I see. The organization I work for doesn't operate in the same way as the kind that you work for," he replied. "There are no demotions for us. But I am familiar with what you're describing."

"I have a friend on the first floor," continued Sam. "He was demoted because he found accounting errors in his company's books. He tried to tell his boss about the discrepancies, but soon after found himself working in the back room sorting receipts all day. He would've looked for another job, but his boss had been stealing from the company, so he wanted to keep my friend close and threatened to sue him, accusing my friend of cooking the books. Since he didn't have the means to defend himself, my friend couldn't do much else but stay. I believe that's what it means to be demoted. I met him under similar circumstances as you and I are meeting today. He was on his fourth letter too."

The tale made me realize that the group was cruel and would use any piece of personal information to its advantage. To wait for a man to be under duress before bringing your attack is as underhanded a tactic as I've ever heard. A man is most crushed when his sense of purpose is vanishing—the perfect time for them to introduce an alternative one.

"He's doing really well now. He's been using the amenities more and spends much of his time outside. I've seen him up and down the road many times since we met. The Headmaster's happy with him too."

My reflexes took over and I couldn't help but let out a small cough just as I was raising the tea cup toward my lips. The warm liquid splashed back on itself, jumping out of the cup, before resting on my face, clothes, and the edge of the desk in front of me. I put the cup down quickly and wiped my face with my gloves, the smell of tea sticking to my nostrils.

Sam stood quickly, and with unabashed sincerity asked, "Are you OK, John?"

I was fine, but I liked seeing him concerned.

"Yeah," I replied.

He sat back down in his chair so slowly that I couldn't tell whether or not he was actually moving. His eyes stayed fixed on mine, as he finally settled into his former position, while firmly gripping his tea cup with both hands.

"Do you really want to start this conversation by talking about the Headmaster?" I said. "Only ignorant people would buy such a farce."

Sam twitched his head slightly sideways and froze in his seat.

"What makes you think that?" he replied, with grave concern in his voice.

As our conversation moved forward, I was trying to form an idea of what type of man I was dealing with. Depending on how well I could read my adversary, I thought, I could leave him with the impression that I wouldn't interfere with their group, or even discuss them with anyone, as long as they ceased harassing me. On the other hand, Sam seemed so genuinely concerned for my well-being that part of me started to think that the request to see me about the conditions of the building was honest, and that for some reason he needed my advice. It came to me just then that he must have looked at my rental application and knew of my standing as a scientist. They wanted to utilize my training to either advance their cause, or maybe because they really did have some issues with the ventilation and needed the expertise of a skilled lab-man.

I was taking a risk because the Headmaster was obviously the leader of their organization and I knew that some cults took it as near blasphemy if you said anything negative about their commander. Suddenly a clever idea hatched in my mind, and I began to think that there might be a way for me to get something out of him. Maybe he had access to the building's supply room, or would allow me to remove the signs outside the apartment. If he was an amateur at manipulating people it wouldn't be hard for me to turn the tables on him. His old friend from the first floor may have bought his performance, but unlike him, I was about to use the charade to my advantage. Either way, after getting to know him briefly, I wasn't all that worried about his influence. I decided to continue playing along and press him for answers.

"Sam, I thought you brought me down here to discuss the condition of the building. I'm not sure which department you work for, but you obviously know my credentials. Do you think you are the first person to try and leverage my training?"

Sam didn't object to my assertion that they really wanted me here because of my training as a scientist, so I decided put my cards on the table.

"Let's cut to the chase. Have you brought me here because I'm a scientist, or because you want my apartment?"

I was careful to read Sam's reaction, and was surprised to see a sadness in his eyes that I hadn't seen yet.

"Neither," said Sam, with a calm voice. "We do want your opinion, not because you're a scientist, but because you're a person. There is a difference, John."

For a moment he sounded like a psychiatrist, and the zig made me feel slightly unsettled.

"Listen, Sam, you seem like a friendly person. I'd like to share my thoughts on how to make this place better, if that's what you're after, but let's do this civilly. First you shove magic tea in my face, then you're talking about your prey on the first floor, and now the

Headmaster—the character you use to scare children. What is this all about?"

He didn't move a muscle, and the sadness in his eyes was now penetrating. I suddenly felt like I was being harsh with the man, and a feeling of embarrassment stirred inside me as I looked at him. I'm not sure why I didn't notice the sorrow he carried when I first sat down with him. I had only spent a few minutes with him, but there was an amiability about him that I hadn't expected, and it felt good to talk with someone, even though he was a stranger. I had spent considerable effort avoiding contact with other people, but Sam was somehow different. His tone was innocent, with a hint of naivety, and I was sure I had the intellectual upper hand in our encounter. I had been afraid that it would be a waste of my time to come down here, and although I suffer to admit it, the brief companionship alone seemed to be worth the trip.

"You've been forgetful for some time, John. Take another sip of tea, and this time focus on its lovely flavors."

His voice suddenly carried the distinction of authority, though not enough to scare me off completely, and I reminded myself not to get to comfortable.

"We do spend a lot of time with children. We find them to be extremely reliable messengers."

"How do you people sleep?" I snapped, involuntarily losing control of my wits. "You know your game won't last forever, right? Power is cyclical."

In that moment, I knew I had lost control. Sam didn't miss a beat, but my outburst probably caused him to reveal more then he should have.

"Oppression is cyclical; power is absolute."

As soon as Sam finished his sentence, I felt a chill go down my spine. His eyes pierced me like a javelin that has successfully hit its target on the first throw. Sam paused for moment before he said, "Do you remember who brought you to this building?"

"Brought me? I have no idea what you're talking about," I replied soberly.

"I see," Sam said calmly.

He sipped his tea slowly, his arms and hands rising and falling from his lap to his mouth with precision. He was like a mechanical drone, deep in thought, while constantly oiling his parts with the flow of warm tea. I didn't know how to explain what was happening just then, but he seemed to grow larger and larger as we sat in silence. The features on his face barely changed, other than when he licked his lips to devour the small traces of liquid that were left behind after each time he had raised and lowered the cup. His hair suddenly stood out the most, as the lightness of the gray contrasted with the grays and blacks of the rest of the room.

I had studied time for decades before meeting Sam—it was my academic area of expertise—and my work had changed the way people think about the subject. My dissertation was called *Time's Accumulating Effect—Something Gained, Nothing Lost.* But even with all of my experience, never had time become so mysterious and unpredictable as it had during these fleeting moments. I felt like I was concrete, unmovable. It seemed that even if I could move, I shouldn't, as though time had stopped for me, but Sam was fluid. It looked as though he were in motion even though he wasn't, and that somehow I was trapped, stuck in a moment in time that Sam was outside of. His eyes grew larger and larger, and I could count the times that he would wrinkle his brow just slightly. The longer I sat there, and the closer I looked, the more I noticed the features on his face move, even in the slightest way. The tiny pores on his cheek seemed to breathe in and out, moving like the chest of a man who is sound asleep. He blinked now and then. When his eyelids closed I could hear them thunder shut with a loud echo, and then suddenly reopen with a squish. His gaze never changed, and I could hear his satisfied rumble every time he moved the tea cup away from his mouth. Even when I tried, I couldn't see past the small features on his face, as if his face had filled the whole room and when I looked up as high as I could, I saw his hair line, and if I looked as far as I could to the right, I could only see as far as his ear with the corner of his right eye in my peripheral. I was paralyzed in time, and my whole world had involuntarily sunk down to the size of Sam's face. I don't know why, but for the first time in as long as I could remember, I felt safe.

3

I don't know if it was another one of his tricks, but before I knew what had happened, he was standing beside me with his hand on my shoulder. He dug his thumb gently into my skin and rubbed it in a circle. I sighed momentarily, and then stood up as quickly as I could. The room seemed to spin before I was steady on my feet.

"I'd like to know why you haven't been using the amenities around the building, and then I'd like to show you something." Sam spoke as though he was talking to himself, and the words came out like a whisper.

Part of me thought that it wouldn't be such a bad thing to indulge Sam just a little, but mostly I couldn't resist his charm. I was beginning to think that he was the one who had created all of the signs that hung around the building; Sam the expert propagandist. I suddenly spoke up without considering whether or not he was beginning to subdue me.

"You know what I'd change first around here?" Sam's eyes squinted, and he looked up and down my face.

"What's that?" he asked in a happy voice.

"I'd put in some ventilation to fix the dingy air. You non-scientific fools don't realize how it could be. I've been studying the cosmos for years and know that the air outside our atmosphere is perfect. There's no hazy fog or worry of contaminants. If we send something up there, it just goes on forever as though nothing could affect it."

"Why don't you to take off your sunglasses?" Sam didn't flinch in his response. His tone was bold, yet flavored with the innocence I'd perceived in him.

"What sunglasses?" I asked.

"The ones that you've been wearing ever since I was assigned to you. You've had them on since you left your position."

"Assigned to me? Left my position?" I almost stammered before I continued, "What is this . . . ?'

I couldn't believe what he had said and was suddenly paralyzed by the complexity of the situation. Could it be possible that Sam, the letters, the cult, and the signs were due to my colleagues. The university where I had been a professor was prestigious and had deep pockets, but this?

Envy can be a vicious toxin that poisons normally highly functioning individuals, and my colleagues were no exception to this sad truth. The fellowship knew my work was exquisite, and that's why they had kicked me out. Were they now trying to get the research papers that I hadn't handed in? If they couldn't understand the truth then, they surely wouldn't now. I knew the faculty had a certain amount of reach and that they would sometimes use underhanded tactics to get what they wanted, but this seemed farfetched by any stretch of the imagination.

I was beginning to understand why Sam was so comfortable around me. He had probably been watching my movements for some time. I also started to think that everything that had happened over the last few years was part of a conspiracy to distract and dismantle me. I had to be more careful in my reactions and hope that Sam would inadvertently reveal the plot.

Sam remained calm for a moment, and then let out a small burst of laughter. It seemed as though he had been holding it in since I had sat down with him. His face crunched together when he smiled, but the sorrow never left his eyes.

"What's the joke?" I asked.

"I'm sorry, I shouldn't have laughed, it's just that . . . "

He patted my back and then rubbed it in circles. He started to hesitate, so I said, "Just that what?"

He had a sincere touch, and it felt for a moment like we were old school chums, caught up in some harmless mischief in the yard. I almost shocked myself by putting my hand around his shoulder in reciprocation, but stopped myself.

"John, you've been putting on the same pair of sunglasses every time you leave your apartment for years now. I don't know if you sleep with those things on, but I wouldn't put it past you."

I was stunned by his direct tone. I realized then that I wasn't sure who I was up against, or who he really worked for, and looked toward my boots in contemplation. When I looked up, Sam was holding up a mirror in his hand that pointed in my direction. The face in the mirror was that of a man wearing a scarf, large coat, hat, and dark sunglasses.

Suddenly, the wide expanse of the basement walls shrank and I felt trapped. My hands started to shake, and anxiety crept up from my toes, slowly making its way to the top of my head. I tried as hard as I could to suppress the feeling, but knew that I had lost to it even before I'd started fighting it. My chest felt like it had thousands of tiny pins sticking out of it, and that someone was running his hands up and down the tip of each one, causing of wave of subtle sensations that weren't necessarily bad, but were certainly uncomfortable. The top of my head was getting warm, and I removed my hat and slumped back into my chair. Had he put something in the tea?

"John, I can't take the glasses off for you, but I've shown you that they're there. I've been through a similar situation with a friend of mine from the twentieth floor. He had ear plugs in for over 25 years and had completely forgotten about them. We put up signs all around his apartment and in the halls leading to the elevator just for him, but he always ignored them. Take them off slowly now; your eyes will need to adjust."

I rubbed the top of my head with my hand and scratched my scalp. I knew Sam was standing right there, but I tried to touch the glasses and confirm their existence without him noticing. I could feel the hard plastic rims and lens just barely through my fingertips as I cautiously moved my hand toward and away from the foreign object. My mind was racing about the faculty, and I tried to recall my last days there. Had they done something to me? Who was to blame for this?

"Slowly now, John," said Sam in a soothing voice.

I finally rustled up enough courage to undo the clip at the back of the plastic frame. I pulled the glasses from my head, and when the scene from the room hit me, time was against me once again. For just a brief moment, I had the feeling that I was a small child. It was firm, but distant. And as quickly as I felt it, and longed for it to stay, the sensation had passed.

The dingy air that I'd been trying to escape from for as long as I could remember had instantly ceased to be. It was as though murky waters had suddenly vanished and been replaced by a crystal clear substance. I didn't want to move. It seemed as though the entire basement was actually a giant piece of perfect glass that had been poured around us, and that Sam and I were fixed in the middle. All of the objects had become clear. The desk now had sharp edges and was in the shape of a perfect rectangle. The corners of the walls that reached to the ceiling protruded from the floor in impeccably straight lines. The chandeliers let off an awesome glow of white, and it burned my eyes to look directly at them. I squinted and looked at the floor, covering the back of my head with my hands, while leaning my torso far into my lap.

"I think I'm going to be sick!" I cried.

Sam was still standing close by, but he had taken a few steps back. I didn't sense his presence anymore, and felt like a rock that was rolling slowly down a hill. My eyes were closed but saw white light, as though the glass box we were encased in had been filled with milk. I wanted the sensation to be over, and cupped my hands around my eyes. Carefully I began to open and close my eyelids. I focused on the ground and used my hands to block out most of the light, allowing more and more to come in as I adjusted to the brightness. My mind flashed with images of the tea I had drunk, and the faculty. When I had regained my orientation, I sat back in the chair with my hands over my eyes and slowly lifted them. I then opened my eyes with the hope that the room would be filled with the same dingy air that I had disdained, but had become so accustomed to.

When I opened them, everything was calm, as though the storm had blown over and a gentle breeze was settling in. Although I wasn't moving, or really thinking about anything, the room was drenched in a sea of excitement. There was a twinkling quality no matter where I set my eyes, and I saw thousands of variations of the same object depending on the way the light reflected off of them. The room was full of vibrancy from the radiating glow of the rainbow created by the chandeliers. It reminded me of the first time I had looked through a telescope and watched the bright burnt umber flashes of the glowing orange sun. But this was more real, as though the room were covered in a thick paste that I could scrape off and hold. I looked around the entire basement, scanning the walls, memorizing what I was seeing. I couldn't be sure when the tea would wear off and I didn't want to leave without committing the sight to memory.

"Good work, John, how are you feeling?"

The sound of Sam's voice brought me back to reality and I quickly recovered as much of my sanity as I could. I'd been drugged by a man who was trying to get my apartment, or worse, who wanted my research papers. I had to pull myself together. I focused my mind, forcing the wonder to subside. I fought to feel like my old self, and grasped the feeling tightly when I found the familiar stability in my mind. I wanted to reach for my sunglasses, but something stopped me. I stood up and started to pace around the desk while continuing to look around the room, confirming to myself that all of my faculties, aside from my sight, were intact. Sam watched as I went around the desk several times.

"I know you're probably in a bit of shock, but we should keep moving. It's not uncommon for people to take the first step and then revert back to what they're accustomed too. What I mean is, John, I want you to break those glasses, and then I want to show you something."

I wasn't sure what to make of Sam's request, but something about him made him very persuasive. Part of me must have been stuck in that trance-like state because before I could process his request, I found myself stomping the sunglasses on the marble floor, breaking them into a thousand tiny pieces.

4

WE BEGAN WALKING QUICKLY. Sam was in the lead and I followed closely behind. The colors seemed to whiz past me and I felt light on my toes without the dingy air around to slow me down. We were heading toward the opposite end of the basement from where I had first entered. Sam walked with a skip in his step combined with a sort of confidence. I found it a bit unsettling to see a man so unashamedly joyful, but it was this same quality that made him so convincing.

The ceiling looked even farther away than it had when I first entered the basement. The crystals from the chandeliers caused the colors that they captured to dance around, and they freely leapt from one crystal to the other. The floor was moving by in a blur, and the greens and oranges and reds that made up the marble palette were swirled together like a bowl of freshly flavored soup flowing beneath our feet.

When I looked back I could see Sam's desk, now a miniature of its original self, centered in the cavernous room. The aluminum panels of the elevator doors in front of us seemed to shimmer back and forth. As we got closer, I could clearly see Sam and myself in the reflection. I thought we must look silly together, as the stark contrast between my dark outfit and his colorful one became evident for the first time.

Sam pushed the up button and the elevator chimed soon after.

"We don't normally take people here, but the Headmaster insisted in your case," Sam remarked as we walked into the elevator.

He looked carefully at his options, and after pondering all of the buttons, he selected the one marked with a C.

"What do you know about time?" Sam asked as the elevator doors shut quietly.

Finally, he had showed me his true intent. Now I was sure that Sam was after my research papers. If he worked for the building, then it made sense for him to know that I was a scientist. My occupation had been on the application form of the lease. But there was no way for him to know that I had studied time while at the faculty. It couldn't be a coincidence.

It all made sense. I had focused most of my attention on the study of time, but had written a myriad of papers on many important topics.

As I picked up more recognition, I noticed that my colleagues began to treat me differently. The symptoms of their envy were subtle at first. Before my best publications, I had been teaching three different courses. This was normal for most tenured professors, and an acceptable arrangement for both parties. After I had published my landmark discoveries on the nature of time, I expected, and rightly so if you ask me, for them to lighten my teaching load. One class would be enough to stoke my knowledge (even published researchers need a bit of human interaction) and challenge the students.

When I approached the members of the fellowship with the request to go down to teaching one class while maintaining my salary, they turned me down. I knew it was an unlikely appeal, but so was my willingness to stay with that particular university, and I thought the compromise would be obvious to them. Instead, their denial was the first sign of their collective affirmation that someone of my talent no longer belonged among them. I submitted to their decision, but through this action they'd tarnished their reputation of extolling high-quality research.

I say the envy started subtly to highlight the fact that it would eventually become intolerable. I didn't mind taking a sip of whiskey in the classroom, but normally saved the delight for between periods. On more than one occasion when I opened my office drawer to remove the bottle, I had found my whiskey to be missing. This in itself didn't seem like something of grave concern, until I began to notice that as often as the bottle was taken, my papers had also been shuffled through. I don't know what kind of dolt they had sent to copy my work, but if he hadn't stolen my whiskey, I probably never would have noticed the scheme.

After that, they trapped me, and the ploy worked perfectly. If I had gone to the office, they would have plagiarized my work, but by doing my research from home, they could fire me for not showing up to teach my classes. When I was finally let go, they had written on the dismissal papers that it was because I had stopped showing up to teach. Now I understood just how far they would go to get my research on the nature of time.

It wasn't the right moment to accuse Sam. I wasn't sure yet who he really was, and if he shut me out, I wouldn't be able to find out exactly what the faculty wanted, or how far they were willing to go to get it. I would continue playing along with the charade and try to carefully turn the situation back to my own advantage. I would engage, but not give him information he could use.

"It's not all that complicated," I said. "Time is basically just a way for us to measure when a certain event occurred in comparison with another event."

The elevator wobbled back and forth slightly and chimed as we moved past each floor. The intervals between the sounds became less and less as we picked up speed.

"I see," said Sam.

His forehead was crunched toward the top of his nose and his bottom lip had raised itself over the top one. The elevator had leveled to a steady rate of ascent, and the chimes had developed a consistent rhythm as we glided upward.

"Not complicated for me, anyways," I said in response to Sam's look of confusion.

The elevator slowed, and then came to a gentle stop. Sam had a large smile on his face now and looked as though he was finished with our conversation. The doors opened and we stepped out onto a large metal bridge with thick iron railings on both sides. Its design was elegant and the room was brightly lit.

26

I looked over the edge of the railings and could see that we were high up in the air. Down below us on the floor were large gears in motion, all of varying sizes, which spun at different rates. They looked to be gold, or bronze, and the large ones moved very slowly while their teeth clicked into place. The gears were stacked on top of each other. There were so many that I couldn't have counted them all if I had tried. I looked ahead and saw that the bridge was separated into two levels by a large staircase. Sam was leaning over the railing watching the gears, nodding his head just slightly to the sound of the large ones as they locked and unlocked from each other. There was a space between the steps of the staircase. Through it, I could see two sets of pendulums moving up and down, in opposite directions, to a constant beat. There were four pendulums altogether, two on the left working side by side, and two on the right.

Sam moved back from the railing and stood upright. He looked at me and when his eyes met mine, I was suddenly afraid. I knew my senses weren't operating at full capacity and braced myself for what might happen next. We were alone on the metal structure and the distance between myself and the gears below was significant. I was overwhelmingly relieved when all he finally said was, "Let's go up."

As we walked toward the staircase, I was struck by the sounds of the gears as they echoed quietly off the ceiling. When we reached the top of the stairs, there were two large clocks looking at us. They were both white with black Roman numerals and large red hands. They stood much taller than Sam and I, and their size explained why the room was so large. Both clocks were identical, other than for one glaring difference. The clock on the left moved in a clockwise direction, while the clock on the right spun in a counter-clockwise direction. Both large hands would hit the number 12 and the number 6 at the exact same time, but for the remaining minute, they were polar opposites. They were startling in appearance, and no one would consider clocks to be beautiful unless they had seen these ones.

After breaking from the hypnosis of the turning hands, I saw that there were two men sorting through two large stacks of paper at the foot of each clock. We stood side by side on the steel frame and watched them closely.

The man on the left was searching through his stack, and after a few moments of flipping through the papers, I saw him pass a paper over to the man on the right. The man on the right took it and started flipping through the corners of his own papers, beginning roughly in the middle of the stack. After he had flipped through about an inch worth of his pile, he slipped the one he had been handed into his stack, and then made sure the new addition was flush with the rest of his pile. The man on the right then seemed to take a break from the action, as the man on the left continued flipping through his papers. After a few moments, the man on the left handed over another one.

We watched the men work with curiosity for a few minutes as we took in the scale of the operation. From my brief observation, I determined that the man on the right sometimes passed papers to the man on the left, but that the ratio of papers going from left to right was ten to one.

I hadn't yet let go of the fact that Sam could be a member of the cult and continued in my struggle to pin point his desires. Was I being paranoid about the faculty? Now that I had seen the lovely clocks, and the men working diligently in front of us, I started to think that our environment didn't seem to support either of my hypotheses.

5

THERE WAS A LONG steel bench facing the clocks a few paces in front of us and Sam sauntered over to sit down while I stayed a couple of feet behind him.

"Well, what do you think?"

I wasn't sure how to answer.

"Can you guess what those men are doing?"

I couldn't have thought of an answer in a million years and stayed silent. Sam waited for the silence to hit bottom before he spoke again.

"Time is not what you think, John."

We continued watching the men work, and this time the man on the right handed a paper over to the man on the left.

"Far from being just a unit of measure, although it is that too, there are actually two different types of time that we experience. There's the kind on the left, and the kind on the right."

Was he trying to bait me into sharing my latest discoveries? First he gave me tea that contained some kind of hallucinogen. Now he's brought me here to impress me by the scale of these mechanical devices so I'll let my guard down and speak more about time.

"I'm not giving you anything," I said coldly.

Sam looked at me with disappointment, and leaned his head to the right. He rolled his eyes, and I felt like I was a small child for the second time that day, only this time I wanted the moment to be over, but it stayed. It was the first time in as long as I could remember that I had the feeling of letting someone down, and I barely knew the man. Something about his character forced me to acknowledge his emotions. My face became a little warm and I caught myself blinking again in rapid succession. I wasn't sure what to say next, or what to think and began to think that the tea was affecting far more than just my sight.

Sam raised his arm slowly and pointed directly in front of himself as he said, "You see those two stacks of paper? The stack on the left is the names of all of the people who aren't on the road."

Confusion began to lower its jaw on my mind, inhibiting me from understanding who he worked for. If he was part of the cult, they were a persistent bunch, Suddenly, I began to understand why there were so many signs around the building, and how they'd been able to infiltrate the minds of all my neighbors.

"Time seems to be moving forward for them. It's as if they're always gaining another second, another minute, and another hour. In their minds, time keeps being added onto their lives, and this has made them stop searching for the road. They think that the longer they have lived, the more time is being piled onto itself, and that because it seems like they have more time than they did a year ago, a week ago, a day ago, or even just a moment ago, that there's no real hurry to find anything. That's why they aren't on the road. They don't realize that they're being crushed by time. In fact, some of the people on the left are so buried in time that they've completely forgotten that there even is a road. That's when people start getting letters from us."

I chuckled to myself out of nervousness, acting as though I was following Sam's logic. The comfort of my apartment was suddenly etched in my mind and I wanted to be there, but had no idea how to get back.

"The people on the right experience time the correct way, the way we are supposed to understand it. For them, time is counting down. When time is counting down, there's an urgency not to waste any of it on unproductive matters. They not only remember that the building will be torn down, but look forward to the new one, and make sure they know how to get there. We've always made it clear that a new, better building is coming, and we've provided the road and the directions. The people on the right know where the new site is, and they're preparing and counting down the days to when they can move in."

For some reason I thought it would be advantageous for Sam to believe I was on his side. I was on his turf, and had to admit to myself that I'd underestimated him somehow.

"Why are more papers moving from the left to the right, than from the right to the left?"

Sam was pleased with the question, and gave me a small wink.

"We're a very active group," he replied with a smile.

"Who's 'we?'" I asked anxiously.

"The ones who work for the Headmaster."

"Right, the Headmaster." I was careful to sound agreeable, but not to agree.

"The people on the left are stuck. They've ignored the signs yes, but there's nothing keeping them on the left. In most cases they became lazy, or forgetful. Time is funny that way, and irrationality does strange things to people. If the idea creeps in that time has always been here, it can really flip people's instincts and diminish their reasoning capabilities. But like I said, nothing is truly keeping them there. They just choose not to see, you see?

"It has always been here. It's been accumulating forever," I said with a resentful grunt, followed quickly by a feeling of regret. This didn't seem like the right time to start a fight.

"Like I said, irrationality can diminish peoples reasoning abilities no matter how smart they are. We take the care of our residents very seriously and that's why we work so hard to move people from the left to the right. Since there's no good reason to be on the left, and plenty of reason to be on the right, we have a very high success rate of switching back to their original thoughts on time."

In my state of vulnerability I tried hard to stay focused and decipher what Sam was trying to explain, but none of it made any sense. Almost anything you can think of can be abandoned, but not time. It has its hands wrapped tightly around everyone, and even though each of us will expire, it's imperative for us to hold onto time aggressively while we can.

I knew control would be at the center of any brainwashing effort. Since moving into the building I noticed that conformity surrounded me on a daily basis. Everyone smiled, and most people were overly polite when I spoke to them. And the signs, the signs were everywhere, designed to crush us into submission. "The road leads to life." "Your fears have been conquered on the road." "You're always welcome back on the road." Part of me understood that the other people simply weren't like me. Avoiding harassment would make them happy. I guess conflict didn't sit well with them, but I was different—intelligence and reason made me different. The road was where they wanted us, and it was appealing to think that being there would suddenly relieve me from the burden of time, but surely that was a lie. Suddenly it all started to become clear.

"Now I understand your methodology," I said with a slight chuckle.

"Well, that's good news."

His smile was gleaming.

"You create a lie so elusive and desirable that people won't, no can't, question it. Sneaky bunch of . . . "

I let my thought trail off and looked to Sam for his reaction. He stared at me now and seemed hurt by my remarks. He wasn't saying anything, but the look on his face shouted for me to withdraw my comments at once.

"How can time be our friend? Aside from your unscrupulous lot, it's our worst enemy. You've never been to a funeral, have you?"

Sam paused before he responded.

"I've been to many."

His tone suddenly became very somber, which led me to believe his remark. But the fact that he'd been to a funeral wasn't enough for me to stop my barrage. I normally forbade myself from feeling a sense of duty, because I knew it was only another way for the people like Sam to steer us in the direction that they wanted us to go, but something inside pushed me to continue.

"Our fate is a shared one no doubt, but that doesn't mean we should embrace it. Piling on time, or better said, convincing oneself to believe it's being piled, is a virtuous undertaking that requires great strength of mind. This is the fittest characteristic we can possess. To exclude the fact of meaninglessness, or in another word, death, and continue anyways. How callous to preach a message of surrender!"

I half expected him to hit me just then, but instead he waited quietly for me to calm my anger. He seemed to be a man of even temperament, and my image of him from that of when we first met was beginning to change. He's demeanor suddenly became very serious. He grabbed my arm softly in his hand and looked me directly in the eyes.

"You're right that we share a similar event, but fate is something quite different. Like it or not, the building is here and you are in it. For this you had no choice. But whether you find the new site, or stay here when it gets torn down, is completely up to you. I'm simply here to show you the way. The decision to ignore the signs or get on the road is only yours to make."

His tactics were far less forceful than I would have guessed them to be. The propagandists were skilled at their trade, and I could see why they'd picked Sam to be their spokesperson. He approached me like a calm, quiet conscience, whispering for my attention.

"Do you really think you can convince me to buy into your cult, and get onto your make-believe road?" I exclaimed mockingly.

Sam exhaled a deep breathe as though he was enjoying a moment of relaxation.

"We're not shy about our tactics and have a variety of methods. One of the most effective ways to begin the process is to get people using the amenities again. We notice that people who appreciate the amenities are far more likely to find their way back to the road than those who don't. And once people start walking down the road again, they rarely go back to the left side."

Sam thought for a moment before continuing.

"Do you remember when you were a child, and your parents would give you a dollar to use at the store? There was no prerequisite when they gave it to you, and you knew they didn't want you to pay them back. They simply gave you the dollar and wanted you to enjoy it. Sometimes you forgot that they gave it to you, then one day, you reached into your pocket on the way home from school and there it was, like it had been giving to you for the first time all over again."

"I couldn't remember being a child if I tried."

"That's what it's like to be back on the road to the new building. It's like remembering that you had that dollar, and you're suddenly grateful and excited to spend it."

I couldn't be sure what all this was for. The large clocks, the men working directly in front of us, the sound of the gears as they clanged beneath our feet. I was suddenly tired of Sam's pressure, and for the fact that he wouldn't come right out and just say what this was really all about. It was probably close to noon and if he hadn't brought me here, I would've been taking my afternoon nap shortly. I wasn't about to give up my freedom, my papers, or listen to his fairy tales any longer. It was time to stop being so kind. I liked the company, but reminded myself of the great effort I had made in protecting myself from being taken advantage of.

"OK, Sam, I think you've had too much of that tea. First of all, I know more about time than you, and you're not talking me out of the fact. These clocks are interesting to look at, and I can see that those men have been hired to do something, but aside from my own knowledge, there's a gaping hole in everything you've told me."

Sam barely raised his voice and replied with the same tone, which had seemed sincere, but now seemed obnoxious, as he had used since I'd met him.

"Oh."

"Have you been outside in the last one thousand years? There aren't any amenities. This place is a waste land, especially compared to what I've seen in my telescope, never mind the insufferable people and the general pain of existence. If you think sending people into the uninhabitable roads of this area, by calling them spectacular amenities, is going to get them to believe there's a Headmaster, and to follow you wherever you tell them to go, you're insane. I don't know if you're trying to fool people, or if you're trying to steal my research, but it's time for you to come clean before I throw you over this railing!"

The events of the morning had been building inside me and they had finally boiled over. Sam didn't react the way I had expected him too. He stayed motionless on the bench as he continued to watch the two men in front of us. The man on the left had paused for moment to glance at the scene, but he seemed assured that Sam had everything under control and got back to his paperwork. The man on the right didn't even look up.

"You don't need to panic, John. Remember, time will be your companion when you make the switch. A countdown is far more regenerative than its opposite, and allows you to wait patiently for what's to come."

His voice was peaceful and soothing, Sam didn't seem worried about anything except enjoying the clocks spin. I could see his eyes follow the dial. I let my nerves calm down just slightly, and copied Sam in what he was doing. The predictability of the sound of the synchronized hands moving along their infinite path was enough to subdue the angst.

"You've brought us right to the topic that I wanted to discuss with you today. The amenities. I see now that your attitude toward them is not all that positive. Can you tell me why you feel this way?" asked Sam, with a sympathetic voice.

"If you had your eyes open you would have no trouble understanding," I said.

"I see," Sam replied, "I thought I was the one who opened your eyes."

The movement in the environment must have had an effect on me because I was suddenly swelling with information and could barely hold my tongue. Part of me wanted to launch an assault of words on this man, but I had learned that small steps are a better way to convince someone. Sam didn't know what I knew, and after being convinced of one's allegiances, I knew I had to take things one step at a time in order for him to understand.

"After you study the cosmos, you begin to understand things about this place," I began to explain. "We've discovered an endless array of inspiring ideas out there—gravity, dark matter, negative energy—it's endless. I'm telling you, Sam, once you know the things I know, you won't look at this world the same way." It felt good to ease Sam into the conversation.

"Yes, the skies are brilliant," he replied. "We often bring the people who we send letters to onto the roof at night, but we knew that wouldn't help your case."

"How long have you been studying the sky?" I asked. "If you've looked at it seriously, then you should know better by now."

"I don't see the connection, John, what is it about the stars that stops you from using the amenities?"

It felt as though we were old school chums again. I was glad that Sam was listening. I wasn't about to say it, but it had been sometime since someone had really listened to me. I didn't think he would completely understand what I was about to share, but it was refreshing all the same. My nerves started to calm even more, and I resolved myself to keep things under control and use the opportunity to show Sam my knowledge. I hadn't been in front of a classroom for some time and had missed the intoxicating sensation of making my thoughts known.

"When we look at the planets closely, we see all sorts of wonderful sights. There's a moon that hovers around Saturn that contained mass amounts of lava in the distant past. We can observe the massive canyons and valleys that it formed. And you know the craters on the moon? We've been able to model the speed of the asteroids that hurdled toward it, before they finally smashed the surface, and left their impression. They would have been teaming with volatility; gases burning, chemicals being spewed, molecules ripping through other molecules. Don't you see, Sam, there's no pain, no problems, no suffering. Just a wonderful array of beautiful objects waiting for us to find them. No murder, no theft, no crime at all. Only meaningful discovery."

He had given me the floor and was listening intently.

"Meaningful discovery?"

"Yes, discovery! And the more we look, and the farther we go, the more discoveries we find. Don't you see the implication?" I paused for a moment and could see that Sam couldn't understand, so I continued. "It doesn't take a genius to understand how broken this place is, and now we know that it's all out there, in the cosmos, not here. By utilizing the cosmos we'll carve a new, perfectly evolved path for humanity! You wouldn't know discovery if it bit you in the . . ."

He stood up before I could finish my sentence. He was shaking his head back and forth while he looked at the ground, and started pacing around a small area in front of the bench. His lips were moving as if he were playing a scene in his head, or trying to piece together a complex puzzle. I had him cornered and he knew it.

"It's time for us to go," he countered. "You know about the clocks, now there's something else I'd like to show you."

Sam raised his hand toward the men who were working and shouted a loud good bye. They both looked toward him and gave a small nod as they continued their shuffling.

6

WE WERE BACK AT the elevator before I realized how closely I had been following Sam's every step. When the doors closed, he pushed the L button before folding his hands in front of him. My pedigree spoke for itself. I wasn't going to say anything else about the conditions of the building until I had Sam's attention again. I would wait patiently for an opportunity to put him in his place, and Sam was on the ropes. Besides, the tea hadn't worn off yet and I was beginning to enjoy looking at all of the colors. I had my faculties together and saw no harm in relishing the drug while it continued to alter my retina. My limbs also felt good, like they'd been stretched for the first time in a long time. My legs felt more firm than they had in years, and the pain in my lower back was subsiding. I felt like an adventurer, who enjoys innocent curiosity for curiosity's sake.

I had no real objective at this point other than to stop the letters and take in the sights. I hadn't tired of Sam's company, and it seemed as though he had no real power. The last thing on my mind was my afternoon nap, and it was rare for me to miss it.

The elevator chimed, but this time the doors stayed close as Sam held the close door button. We stood close to each other and he turned to look at me.

"John, when you use the elevator on your end of the building, go to the second floor and walk to the end of the hall to get back here. Remember, the amenities are for everyone to use and we encourage it."

Without thinking, I asked, "Why doesn't your elevator have any numbers?"

"Our elevators are only used by employees of the Headmaster, and it's not our taste to number everything. We prefer to describe things for what they are." He continued to speak with a contagiously joyful tone. "And John, take off your gloves and your hat. You can leave them here and we'll get them back when we leave."

Without giving it a second thought, I listened. For some reason, the farthest thing from my mind was contamination. Sam pushed the open button and when the elevators doors disappeared into the walls it was like we had released a capsule. The air was suddenly very light and one could almost say it had a certain taste. I started gulping it in by taking large deep breathes in quick succession. I was also hit by a wave of smells that seemed to circle my body and swirl around my head. I would want one smell to stay just a moment longer, but it would be gone in an instant before being replaced by another pleasant aroma. It was a bit exhausting to gulp the invisible liquid while trying to hold on to just one scent. I could tell the scents would keep coming, and that the air wasn't running out, but I instinctively wanted more of each. The more I tried to grasp each one, the farther away they seemed. I must have been standing in the elevator for minutes, and been a real sight, because Sam felt the need to put his hand on my shoulder and reassure me that everything was OK.

"Don't try to have it all at once," he said. "These amenities aren't going anywhere."

He put his hand on my back and gently pushed me toward the exit. I shuffled my feet slowly toward the crack between the elevator and this new world that Sam had brought me too.

Just then I noticed where one of the smells was coming from. As I reached the edge of the elevator, I could see hundreds of tiny green vertical bars sticking up from the ground. They were only an inch or so tall and very flat. The tips of each one looked sharp like a razor. The closer I got to the edge, the more of them I saw. There were thousands upon thousands of these deadly contraptions.

What a deception, I thought to myself. He wasn't planning on reasoning with me at all; he was indeed going to use force. The air must have been contaminated with something and the smell was meant to draw me out. I had to put my gloves back on.

"I'm not going out there!" I exclaimed as I rushed toward the back of the aluminum compartment.

My back banged up against the wall and I tried to squish myself through to the other side. When I felt that Sam was about to make his move on me, he stepped out of the elevator and onto the green surface. The blades bent beneath his feet and it looked as though he was walking on the air. I could see each piece bend under his weight and then spring back up delightfully as he moved around. Contrary to expectations, his steps made no sound at all as he floated over the surface.

"You see, John, it's good."

I looked down toward the corner of the elevator and saw my gloves stacked neatly beside my hat. I wanted to put them on, but something stopped me. I suddenly became aware of my inferior posture and stood up straight, careful to make sure the back of the elevator wasn't too far behind me yet. The smells began to pull me forward and without further hesitation, I bravely walked through the doors and onto the blades.

The ground sank beneath my feet. With my shoes planted firmly in one place, I moved my knees up and down. Everything was secure. I bent down and rubbed my hand across the blades. They tickled me and deposited moisture onto my hand. As I looked closer, I could see the faint outline of Sam's footprints carved into place. The blades had bent under his weight and were now fighting their way back upwards to resume their proud position.

I could feel something warm on my face, but this time it wasn't internal. I wanted to lie down and got down to my knees to further inspect the foreign landscape.

When I glanced up, Sam's feet occupied my entire field of vision. He had taken off his shoes and was standing right next to me.

"You should take yours off too," he said.

I could see the moisture bouncing off the bottom of each foot as he walked away from where I had knelt down. I couldn't resist the suggestion and removed my boots and socks. I didn't know where Sam had taken me, but as I looked around I was struck by how odd this place was. I hurried up to Sam's pace and took in the sights as we glided along.

We were in a wide open space. There were no walls, and although nothing seemed symmetrical, everything seemed to fit.

Large brown towers topped with what can only be described as strange-looking wigs rose all around us. The wigs were emerald and jade and they bounced around like toupees that weren't securely fastened to their skinny-headed wearers. Each strand of hair moved separately from the rest, but together they made a cohesive cover.

At first it seemed that the towers had outdone everything around them in terms of beauty, and would receive the most attention, until I noticed that beneath them a bright variety of colors were basking in the shadows. Crimson, scarlet, and deep lush purple spots lined the ground around each tower. Their round shapes popped off the brown background, while they remained nestled in the green blades that surrounded them. Each one shot a distinct smell toward us, overpowering the scent of the blades as we walked past.

It was as though my sense of smell had been surrounded by a bunch of Robin Hood-inspired henchmen who were were incessantly shooting arrows of aroma at me. I wasn't sure if I was seeing things or not, but the closer I looked, the more I could see small black dots moving back and forth around the tops of the colorful circles. Other than the black flying dots, most of the scene was stationary, but every piece of it seemed to be breathing in and out, dancing to its own lively tune.

The thought of my early years in school flashed back to me. A clear picture of my old elementary school classmates formed in my mind. The faces of several of them were clearly visible, and a distinct emotion followed as I ran through each one. The images flashed quickly and each time I pictured a different face, we were in a different location. Each one was speaking to me, as though I had started the conversation and they were replying, but I couldn't hear what they were saying and only saw their mouths move. I could guess at their mood by the look in their eyes, which was substance enough to remember a deep feeling of joy and freedom. Then, as quickly as it had come into my mind, the memory vanished.

As we walked along, I was continually hit by an unpredictable wave of sensations that I couldn't really describe. It was usually instigated by a sudden smell or gulp of air. When it happened, my whole body suddenly felt as though it were under pressure, as though something from above was pushing me down slightly. It wasn't a bad pressure, and its intensity was strong because the pressure wasn't just applied to one part of me, but equally throughout my entire being. Every finger joint and muscle was suddenly leaned on by an invisible force. What made it special was that the reaction was completely involuntary and impossible to predict or hold onto.

Just then, a black and red cylinder flew over my head, swooping through the sky, just barely avoiding a collision with my skull. I ducked low and out of the corner of my eye saw another cylinder whirl past me, followed quickly by two more. I dropped to the ground, scurrying toward the cover of one of the towers.

Sam had sprung his trap to soon. If we had walked only a few more steps he would have had me in the open and I wouldn't have been able to find cover in time. I looked back toward the elevator and realized that I was too far away to make a run for the enclosure. Besides, now that I knew Sam had people helping him, I could be sure that the elevator was inoperable. I was trapped and had to think of something quickly. I understood now why Sam had gained so much ground on me. He was well ahead of me, which could only be because he needed to avoid being impacted by mistake. He had stopped now and was looking in my direction, but he was far enough away that he wouldn't be able to see whether I'd been hit, or if more cylinders would have to be thrown. This gave me time to make a move. I stayed low and shuffled backward across the soft green blades, desperately trying to decide what to do.

As I inched toward one of the towers, I felt something hard, which had moved when I rolled my hand over it. The sensation alarmed me, and I moved my hand to a different spot on the ground, where I felt another solid object. It wasn't very large and I could easily pluck it from the blades. I was struck by the profoundness of my luck, and found four of the objects in total, collecting them quickly. I decided I would use them to hurt Sam, but I had to find out how many people were helping him, and where they were located, before I committed any of the hard gray spheres to battle.

I sat with my legs sticking straight out and my back against the tower. Sam was motioning for me to stand and had a large smile on his face. He was trying to draw me back into the open. I squeezed a sphere in my right hand and looked around carefully. My fist clenched the object tightly and I shuffled it into the best throwing position based on its size and shape.

"Are we taking a taking break, John?" called Sam. "Fine, that's fine. Lovely, isn't it? There's still something I want to show you, so let's not stop for too long."

Just as he finished talking, I saw two more back and red cylinders fly through the air. This time, to my surprise, they almost hit Sam. I expected to hear them thud as they hit the ground behind him, but instead, they stopped over Sam's head, hovered there for a moment, and then flew straight up into the air, making a high pitched sound as they went. Sam didn't seem concerned at all, and rather than find cover, he whistled back at the departing projectiles.

"Red winged black," Sam said just loud enough for me to hear. As he peered into the blank sky, the projectiles were now two distant black spots. I wasn't sure what to think when I saw four more cylinders whiz through the sky, swooping in all directions. One stopped on one of the brown towers within a few feet of Sam. I stared at the object closely, enthralled by its disregard for obeying the rules, and could see now that I wasn't looking at a cylinder at all, or any other kind of projectile. The object had legs and a mouth. It moved its head from side to side and up and down as it let out quiet little chirps. I was stuck in a trance by its appearance. Does it realize how good the air is, and smell the aromas I'm smelling?

I thought to myself. Then, as quick as it had landed, it whooshed away, and like the others became a black speck in the sky.

I rose to my feet and dropped the spheres from my hand. I was hoping Sam hadn't seen what I was holding as I walked toward him and his seductive smile. I didn't want Sam to know it, but I was beginning to think that I'd gotten myself in way over my head.

7

WE CONTINUED WALKING, SAM always several paces ahead of me, until we reached a point where the brown towers formed a boundary that seemed to stop us from going any farther. The towers were clustered together tightly and Sam came to a halt when he reached the barrier. As I walked toward Sam, I thought that we must have gone as far as we could. He was still ahead of me, but as I got closer to where he was standing, I could see that the brown towers actually had spaces between them, and the spaces seemed to correlate with the awkward width that the wigs stuck out on each side of each tower. The spaces looked black, as though we had reached to end of this place and if we went past the edge, we would walk into outer space. I knew this couldn't be true, but was struck by my desire to know more about the emptiness.

I contemplated the blackness for a moment, when something about the mysterious space gave me a sudden sense of fear. The vast darkness of the universe had always been removed from my direct experience because of its distance. The tools we used to study it had brought it stunningly close to reality, but there was always a counterfeit layer in the way. As colleagues, we longed for this boundary to be broken and vigorously imagined the idea of one day lifting the impediments between this place and what we see out there. We reveled in the thought of leaving the drab corner we inhabited to find our freedom in the endless array of darkness. When I turned off all the lights in my apartment, it would form a sort of blackness, but the space was so familiar that it lacked the mystique of the unfamiliar blackness we saw through our lenses.

The place where I now stood was completely different than anywhere I'd been before. And now that I was in a place I'd never been and could almost touch something so black that so closely resembled what I had longed to occupy, I could barely face it. The void that filled most of the sky had once enthralled me with its seductive promise for more, but when I looked between the towers, I shivered, and could only think to describe its quality as—nothing. I had suddenly become very frightened, but felt a slight relief from the sensation as I realized that with every step I took, I got a little closer to Sam.

When I reached him, I was glad to know that he must not have recognized my state of anxiety because he didn't mention it at my arrival. Instead, he seemed to peer amusingly between our tall vertical acquaintances. I wondered how he dared to get so close to the void, but now that I had reached the barrier, I could see that the light, although slightly dulled, had overpowered the darkness. If exiting the elevator had revealed a whole other world to explore, entering the cover of the towers echoed that sentiment.

When Sam noticed that I was standing right beside him, he looked through the cracks of the towers one more time and then said, "You first, John."

I couldn't be sure yet what Sam intended by having me go first. I was getting tired of trying to determine his motives, but told myself to remain vigilant for a little while longer. Every so often I would forget how far away I was from my apartment and that my only purpose for visiting Sam was to stop the letters from coming.

I didn't respond at first and decided to make a closer inspection of where he wanted me to go before committing myself to the void. I peered between the bases of the towers and rubbed my chin. The wigs had released many of their strands onto the ground, but without making much of an impact on their fullness or form. Most of the strands had changed color, but many of them matched their origins. I was beginning to learn that looks can be deceiving, and although the strands looked more deadly than the blades had, I couldn't perceive an immediate threat. Something told me that the strands would react similarly to the blades when I stepped on them, and I dared myself to take the first stride.

When I finally began to move, a thunderous crunch arose from beneath my feet. I was astounded by its intensity as it was much louder than anticipated, and it didn't seem like the volume in relation to action was remotely possible. The noise encouraged me to continue moving forward. As I went, I expected the sounds to get quieter, but they didn't. I began to pick up my pace and the pleasure of the crunch slowly overtook my mind before becoming my only thought. Once I was completely consumed by the deafening sound of my steps, I stopped abruptly. The silence then became its own sound, reassuring me that I could enjoy the crunch on command.

I looked back to assure myself that Sam wasn't too far behind me, but my pace must have been much quicker than his because I was well ahead of him by now. The crunching sound must have been distracting me because when I took my eyes off of Sam, I noticed for the first time the elegance of our sheltered region. The first thing that struck me was that the towers and wigs were far more interwoven than they seemed to be from afar. Their form was orderly and yet a complete mess all at once. The towers, which looked to be perfectly vertical, actually climbed in all directions and were made up of hundreds of other towers. There wasn't a single angle that any one of the towers hadn't covered. The wigs followed suit by attaching themselves awkwardly to the top of each one. When I first saw them, I was stunned by the brilliance of just one of the objects, but now I could see that each one was made up of hundreds more.

I wasn't sure where to look, and couldn't stop myself from staring deep into the tiniest aspect of the bond between tower and wig. I found the wigs blended well with some of the towers, but contrasted heavily with others. In both cases, they obviously formed one body, and each part belonged closely to the other.

The next thing I noticed was that the air had a fullness to it, but in a way quite different from the air in the building. It was refreshing and carried the blended smell of the wigs, blades, and circles all at once. It was heavy, and although it was invisible, I could feel that I was touching it, or that it was touching me. Every so often, I'd notice a cloud of cooler, lighter air hanging in the way, caught between up and down. It was like a new flavour had been added to the mix.

Suddenly, I realized how many of the towers were surrounding me and felt the fear crawl back into my toes. Sam had almost caught up with me now and I wished for him to hurry. I took a couple of steps, looking in all directions, trying to distract myself with the sound of the crunch. I was shocked to see that Sam had one of the small towers in his hand and used it to steady himself as he walked.

"You shouldn't touch those!" I exclaimed loudly to make sure he could heard me over the sound of his own crunch.

"Touch what?" asked Sam as he approached.

"The towers," I explained. "I don't think they're for touching."

Sam stopped beside me.

"They're not going to hurt you, if that's what you're afraid of," he answered calmly.

He handed the tower over and I took it from him with both hands. It was lighter than expected and had a nice smell. I swung it back and forth in my hand, with the heavy end pointing down, and its momentum seemed to hijack my efforts to keep it moving.

"I don't know where you got the courage—I wouldn't have dared to grab one," I said.

I had to admit that I found the environment very intriguing. I thought the compliment was a sure way to get Sam to continue showing me around, and felt pleased with myself for sprinkling it into the conversation.

"How did you know it was OK?" I asked.

Sam seemed surprise with my question.

"What would make you think that it wouldn't be OK?"

He looked perplexed.

"I don't like people touching my things," I said. "Especially when I've spent hours crafting them."

I thought of my colleagues at the faculty for a moment, and when I saw that Sam's expression hadn't changed, I continued.

"I don't know who put these here, but trust me, if I came up with the design, I wouldn't want anyone going near them."

Sam still wasn't following my logic, so I went on.

"Let's say I create something beautiful. You have the right to acknowledge its beauty, but you don't have the right to claim it as your own. You might feel threatened and project your own abilities onto its existence. But discovery is not the same as creation, and you should be careful not to blur the two."

I thought Sam was enlightened by my comment because he suddenly perked his head up and smiled at me. I got the sense that his brain was turning, and after he considered my thoughts for a few more moments, he said, "You're quite right in a sense, John. What right do we have to anything other than what we can create on our own? It seems reasonable to think that anything beyond ourselves is not ours at all."

"Exactly," I exclaimed. "People need to learn to produce for themselves and stop using things that aren't theirs."

Sam seemed pleased with my response and nodded in agreement.

"How do we reconcile it when we take what's not ours and use it?" he then asked.

"Unless it's clearly given to us, we shouldn't make any assumptions about what belongs to us and what doesn't, but if something is given to us to use, we'd better be grateful."

I didn't need to hesitate at all in my response. The answer was instinctive to me, but for some reason Sam needed it to be explained.

"It's also important to acknowledge the gesture when asked about it by others. There's nothing worse than when someone takes credit for something they didn't do themselves."

"I couldn't agree more," Sam replied.

He bent down and picked up another one of the towers that was lying on the ground beside him. As he moved his feet, I could hear the crunch he produced, but it wasn't quite as loud as when

I stepped. Suddenly, Sam put his hand on my shoulder and cautioned me to be still. I was confused by the gesture, but he repeated himself frantically with a soft whisper.

"You don't want to scare it," he said delicately.

Sam raised his arm slowly and pointed, but without stretching his arm all the way forward. I didn't see anything at first and was paralyzed by Sam's sudden change in demeanour. I didn't know what was happening, but knew enough to hold still. Even with Sam standing next to me, I felt fear wrap its arms tightly around my body. Just then, the towers began to move slowly back and forth as though they had sensed my despair and would now capitalize on my weakened state. I shuddered slightly as the wigs at the top of the towers began whistling down toward us. I was suddenly cold and slightly nauseous.

"Do you see it?" asked Sam very quietly.

He hadn't moved a muscle and his voice held an even tone.

"See what?" I must have said it louder than Sam expected, because he shushed me again.

"Right there," he whispered.

I focused my eyes in the direction that Sam was pointing. I somehow knew that it was very important to listen to his every instruction.

Then suddenly, something appeared, as though the air had taken objects from its surroundings and molded them into something entirely new. It moved slowly in front of us. The figure was still blending into the background as though it wasn't fully formed yet, but was currently being shaped. It was very large with four long legs and its head had large jagged towers sticking out from the top of it. The towers were discolored and looked to be designed as weapons.

The outline of the limbs and the weapons on its head convinced me of the creature's presence, but its body was still part of the towers. Sam still hadn't moved an inch and when I moved my head slightly toward him, I could see happiness in his eyes. I carefully considered my options. Sam and I had been getting along fine and I wondered if I'd let myself trust him more than I should have.

I wanted to stay close to Sam, but the smile on his face couldn't be overlooked—he was up to something. I decided that my best option was to run. I knew the elevator was a long distance from where we stood, but I had no other choice. Once I was back at the building, I would be safe, and if I didn't make it, at least I had tried.

I looked quickly to the left and then to the right. I wanted to plan my escape route without mistakenly running into a trap that could have been waiting for me at the rear. It was as though I was one with the creature because as soon as I moved, its entire body flinched and it looked in our direction. I froze where I stood and was stunned by how quickly it followed my movement. It was staring at us now and I braced for it to charge. The thought of time whisked through my mind for an instant, but I couldn't hold onto it. After a couple of seconds, the large creature leapt into the air and when it landed, it sprinted in the opposite direction from where we stood. Its back legs kicked up higher than its front legs and its white tail waved at us as it rushed away.

My head felt light and my body released a deep sense of fear, which I was now relieved to know was unwarranted. I felt more alive than I had in as long as I could remember. I didn't want the feeling to stay, but was somehow glad that it had come. Sam gently pushed me to the side playfully.

"You weren't supposed to move," he said with a friendly voice.

I was shaking now and Sam quickly picked up on my symptoms.

"Everything's more real out here, isn't it? But in a good way."

I tried to cover up my thoughts and elude his inquiry. The fear that normally followed me around had been heightened by our experience. Other than for a few fleeting instances, which I could barely remember, it was always active. And I don't necessarily mean the kind of fear that's caused by an event, but the kind that creeps up involuntarily and without any cause. I could clearly recall that it had subsided for the few days before and following my graduation. The same clarity also seemed to come when I'd written some of my best papers.

Fear's clutch was so encompassing that for a while, it was the only thing I could think about. I had decided to investigate it further, and it had become one of my secondary fields of study. I was most excited about the project, not only because of its universal nature, but because I thought I'd discovered a few sure-fire ways of defeating it. A trend began to develop in which a relationship existed between my ambitions being fulfilled and my fear fading. I'd waited some time before I'd decided to write on the topic, because as soon as I thought I had discovered the sequence of how to squash the fear, it would creep in unannounced and foil whatever plan I'd developed.

When my system of relating successes and ambitions as a way to conquer it had failed, I turned to understand the source. I thought if I could find out where fear came from, I could overcome it by confronting it at the root cause. I reasoned that my earlier attempts were acting as a band aid, and I needed to understand why fear existed in the first place. After spending serious time on the matter, it became apparent that fear was completely illogical, and although I knew from experience that it existed, the origin of the relentless pressure certainly couldn't be explained.

Fear is simultaneously definitive yet inexplicable, and that's not a good conclusion for a research paper. It's similar to awe, joy, right and wrong, justice, honor, and even love. These are unnecessary traits that our minds have invented, unless you think that Plato was right, or believe in all that supernatural stuff which contends that these concepts are objectively true. Eventually I came to accept fear, as I knew everyone had to at some point.

The encounter with the creature must have sharpened my mind slightly because when I reflected on the day, I conceded that fear hadn't been with me for much of it. I wasn't sure what had forced its absence, but it had certainly come back with a vengeance.

"Sure, more real in a good way," I responded with a slight stammer in my voice.

8

SAM DIDN'T SEEM FAZED by our encounter and walked ahead of me without a care. I found the way he had been reacting to the events that had unfolded during the day to be rather peculiar. I hadn't seen him agitated once since we had met and wished I could say the same for myself. I was beginning to feel more comfortable around him, and began to think that even if he was trying to persuade me to fall in line, he was going about the whole thing in a very non-confrontational way. This put me even more at ease. I decided that it wouldn't do me any harm if I asked him a couple of questions and conjured up some courage. I hurried to catch up and as we walked side by side, I asked, "What's your secret?"

I made the assumption that he would understand the question. It was clear after the short time we'd spent together that he rarely wavered in his confidence, if ever, and that I had more delicate tendencies than he did.

Sam squinted his eyes momentarily. He seemed unsure how to answer.

"Secret?" he asked.

We continued walking and I found the movement to settle my nerves.

"You don't seem to get very anxious about anything. How do you do it? There must be an elixir you could share."

The last part of my question was caused by nervousness. Part of me hoped that Sam had a solution he could share, but I knew it was a long shot even before I asked.

"Anxiousness and fear only swallow people when they're not on the road," he replied. "They will bite at the heels of people on the road, but will never envelope them. It's similar to things like greed and jealousy."

This man is relentless, I thought. But when he spoke, he made me feel like I was the unsettled one. This time, rather than contemplate his sincerity, I decided to face the topic head on. I had been avoiding any possibility that what Sam said had any merit at all, but by this time he had worn me down. His devotion and consistency couldn't be overlooked.

"That doesn't make any sense. These are universal attributes—they can't be escaped."

"It's true they exist, but only as an abnormality. They're only a result of people getting off of the road."

What Sam was saying couldn't be right. Everyone I'd ever known had experienced the attributes we were describing and although people don't like to admit it, I was sure anyone would corroborate the fact that most of our days are spent succumbing to, or trying to resist, these pesky characteristics. Of course, I had never asked anyone directly who had supposedly been on the road. How could I? Until today I was utterly convinced the whole idea was just a scam. I hadn't responded to Sam's statement and he must have sensed that I didn't believe his retort because he felt obliged to expand on his comment.

"Imagine a train, John. What is its purpose?"

He had asked the question abruptly, but I was glad that it was one I could easily answer, and so I responded to it in a similar fashion.

"To get things from one place to another."

"And does it serve any other purpose than to move people and objects from one place to another?"

I wondered if he was trying to trick me, but the question was straight forward.

"No, it only has one purpose. To carry objects or people from one place to another."

"And what good is a train if it's not on its tracks? Can it carry objects or people from one place to another?"

"It's useless."

"If the train knew it was a train, and that it was designed to move from one place to another carrying objects or people, and that it had been taken off of its tracks, how do you think it would react?"

"Unless it enjoyed rotting in the bone yard, I think it would object to its purposeless state of existence and hope to be placed back on the tracks or dismantled at once."

I enjoyed talking as though trains were people. The picture of a train with personality was vivid in my mind, and it exercised my brain nicely.

"We're the train, John," he replied. "Designed with a purpose, and when we leave the track, we're left with nothing. Our subconscious knows this and attacks us with fear and anxiety because we're not where we're meant to be. Our only opportunity is to find our way back to the tracks or slowly rust away as the other trains whiz past."

Sam's comments intrigued me, but the way he described things made them sound too good to be true. I always believed these attributes to be a false conception, invented by our subconscious as a matter of survival. I could never understand exactly how they could contribute positively to my prolonged existence, but reconciled that they were in essence, unreal. A simple spin-off that no longer had grounds for remaining, but that lingered from times past. It's one of the reasons we had to find our meaning in the cosmos, to finally rid ourselves of these poorly evolved qualities.

Over time, I came to realize from the strength of their grips that this couldn't exactly be true. When the pain wasn't present, it was easy to prescribe it as false and explain it away as an unnecessary phenomenon. But when I was experiencing pain firsthand, it was more real and potent than most other things in life. Only a man with no empathy at all, when not in a position of pain, would condemn the rest of us to being fools.

For a while I found cleverness and work ethic to be an antidote to the experience of suffering, but there was no denying that it was never completely quenched. When I was at the faculty, I had learned that fear, anxiety, pain, and jealousies are ever present.

My brain kept telling me that success was the way to overcome suffering, but when I finally pushed the other faculty members out of my way, allowing me to rise to the top of my profession, the emotion of guilt assaulted me for months. I finally had to relent by filling guilts appetite with whiskey, but the guilt was only replaced by some other diabolical characteristic.

As a race, we could all attest to the existence of the internal pain, but no one had ever been able to pin point its origin. I was starting to wish there really was a road. Such a well-crafted ploy, and Sam made it all sound so appealing. But the fact that I hadn't thought of it myself made the whole thing somehow detestable. Though, if we really did have purpose, I could stop trying to invent one.

We continued on in our pace when I suddenly felt a sense of relief. It was as though an academic burden was being lifted, and it allowed me to enjoy the sights and sounds of the strange environment. The towers had become sparse as Sam and I were talking and we had walked through a shallow gully. I could see that they started to become dense up ahead and the darkness appeared once more. I let myself speed up and began walking ahead of Sam.

For some reason I felt compelled to face the black void on my own this time and tried to gain more and more ground on him as we got closer to it. He was a few paces behind me now. When I reached the point where the darkness stayed dark and I couldn't see the objects that I knew would suddenly appear, I forced myself to continue walking without slowing at all. I moved my head back and forth, looking frantically for something to reveal itself through the towers while I tried to maintain outward composure. The towers were crowded much closer together than they were where we had entered. I had to muster all of my abilities to understand where the path was and stay focused on it without stopping or falling over.

As I plowed between the towers I realized that they were bunched so tightly together that I had to spread the skinny ones apart with my hands to squeeze between them. I didn't hesitate and the maneuver worked just as expected. I stomped my way forward and felt the towers scratching the back of my neck. As I walked, the inadvertent rubbing against the towers caused the wigs to drop their strands on my head and I could feel them sticking in my hair. The towers seemed to latch themselves onto to me as I brushed past them, but they never grabbed me so tight as to prevent me from moving forward.

I must have been holding my breath the whole time and when I couldn't muster any more strength, I stopped in my tracks. I couldn't see or hear Sam. The area was dead quiet and I could hear the sound of each strand as it fell slowly through the air before resting on the ground. I suddenly started to panic, now completely alone, and spun my head in all directions, before allowing myself to succumb to my own dread. The towers touched my arms gently and I was completely surrounded. I took a deep breath and let myself take in the atmosphere when I was suddenly overcome with peace.

I let the moment wash over me, careful not to move until the company of peace had completely passed before I decided to continue. I brushed the towers to my left and right, clearing a path down the middle of them. It took some effort to maneuver my way through their grip and with the work came a deep satisfaction.

When I finally made it through the last few barriers I was moving with so much force that I tumbled onto the ground from the momentum, rolling across the green blades. I was back in an open space, similar to the one I had been in when I'd first left the elevator. I wasn't sure how he beat me, but Sam was already standing on the other side and he looked as though he was waiting for me.

I got back to my feet before Sam said, "I know it's different from the cosmos, but what do you think? Can you remember what it was like when you were a young boy and played out here every day?"

Sam had broken the spell. My form seemed to become less solid in the moment.

"You don't know what my childhood was like!" I proclaimed.

"Of course I do, John," replied Sam in an even voice. "I always research the people I've been assigned to."

"Then you mixed up your paperwork. I've never been out here before!" I explained angrily.

"Oh John," Sam chuckled lightly, and respectfully. "You used to be out here every day. It's why you became a scientist, remember. My documents use the term 'enamored by life' to describe your state of mind back then. You know you're still the same person, right? Remember, time is counting down. You don't get more character, added to your character over time, you just gain knowledge which enhances and refines the character you're born with. You can't lose your character either. But like I explained earlier, you can lose your perception when you think time is spinning the other way. It's a difficult concept for people to understand. The Headmaster knows this; that's why he's got us working so hard."

My ear tingled as Sam said "enamored by life." I didn't have blue eyes, but it was as though Sam took a photo of me and when I looked at it, my eyes were blue. It felt as though the deepest layer of my mind had been infiltrated. I had buried ideas into my farthest passages and could suddenly feel them escaping. I had learned to hold my most intimate thoughts tight and felt naked when Sam snapped them up with his powerful imagery.

I had to go on the offensive to save what I was losing. I couldn't be sure what the road was really used for and if there was a Headmaster, why he would want me to be on it. But to use my upbringing as a way to disarm me was an unfair move, even if he somehow knew what I was like growing up.

"If there is a Headmaster, why would he care how I understand time?"

I was hoping Sam didn't think that I'd conceded.

"Because he's the one who made it, and he wants you to enjoy it properly," he answered calmly. "He not only runs the building, he's also the one who put you here."

"That doesn't make any sense. Why would he have made time like a trap? You say he cares for the residents, so then why would he try to confuse us?"

"People mix things up all the time, John. The concept is straight forward to him, but people sometimes find a way to make things difficult. Since we have a tendency to come off of the road, he gave us limited time. For those who aren't on the road, it's supposed to give them a sense of urgency to find their way back. It all has to do with what people call pride. Humans are the only creatures that know that they exist. The Headmaster didn't want people to simply be; he also wanted them to interact from a conscious state with him and with the things he made. The dilemma is that consciousness is a very powerful attribute. Sometimes people get stuck and can't think past their own realization of existence. This leads to all sorts of trouble. It's not supposed to be a means to its own end, but when people don't understand the concept, they lose perception. We were made with power, but we tend to be impressed too easily and simply settle only for ourselves, forgetting everything and everyone."

Sam paused for a moment and I could hear the sound of several red wing blacks, as Sam had called them, calling in the distance.

"It's understandable how it starts. It's impossible to get around the fact that people know they exist—otherwise they wouldn't be creatures capable of consciousness. Sometimes people want to remind themselves that they know they exist, so they'll indulge in pleasures to stimulate the sensation of existing. Of course, being a creature that is conscience is stimulating enough, but the pride of life tells them they need more, so people overindulge until they get lost in desiring pleasures.

"Another example of pride, which is often related to being lost in pleasures, happens when people interact with each other. People often feel inclined to let other people know that they know they exist. This is pride at its basic level, but there's no end to how clever it can become. It begins with a lack of appreciation for existing, which leads to envy toward another person, which leads to jealousy, and a need to brag. It's like people are competing for something that no one will ever win, because they already have the only thing worth competing for, and that's life itself. In the case when pride occurs in an interaction, the behaviour is usually foreign for the recipient at first, but it can spread like a weed. It's foreign because the person who is being forced to acknowledge the existence of the other already knew that the other existed. This makes them question whether or not their own existence and importance is known, making them think that if the other person has to confirm their existence by bragging, then they might too. And so the cycle begins."

"What does pride have to do with time?" I asked. Sam was beginning to weave a deeper spell than the one he was supposed to be pulling me out of.

"Once people get trapped by their own consciousness, they stop using it to interact with the Headmaster and the amenities and start using it to create their own false realities. The fundamental problem is that these realities only exist in their own minds and often conflict with the actual world they're living in. They usually start with time, because people think that if they can flip it around, they can control it and gain more. This would give them more of it to spend on their own fictitious creation. Once time gets flipped, there's no end to the distortion. That's why I showed you the clocks earlier and why we encourage people who are going backwards to begin using the amenities again. The amenities are a window into the house of the Headmaster. They have the ability to pull people out of their own consciousness and back into the real world because the amenities are beyond themselves. It's not the only way to get beyond oneself, but it's a good place to start."

I felt dizzy again, and pictured the safe haven of my apartment. The windows were closed tightly and the fresh paint job was nearly complete. I longed for my afternoon nap and felt confused by what Sam was talking about. For the first time since I had met him, I got the sense that that this whole charade wasn't a charade for him at all. He really did want me to come here and not because he wanted something in return, or because he was trying to force me into submission. He truly cared about this place, and I was starting to think he also cared about me. I had never met a grown man who was as convinced that something was true as I was convinced it was false.

I decided then that the best thing for me to do was to wait for the tea to wear off and keep my mouth shut until he led me back to the building. Sam could drag me around for a while, but I had no reason to truly interact with him along the way. The day would be over soon enough. Sam must have sensed that something was amiss because he grabbed my hand and closed his around it. For some reason I felt a strong urge and so I clenched his hand tightly in return. For a brief moment, I felt like a little boy who has just been taught about the intricacies of life by his father.

"Let's keep moving—the spot is right over here," said Sam and he pulled me forward as he continued walking.

9

WE SAUNTERED ALONG WHILE my mind danced with ideas, and as we walked, I saw plenty of sights that I could barely begin to describe. I was hounded by colors, sounds, and things that moved but didn't breathe, and things that breathed by didn't move. I was trying to resist Sam, but he had a vast array of knowledge and explained many things about what we were looking at. He repeatedly pointed out that we are stewards of the amenities and that we should take care of them as best we can. He said everything we saw was connected and that each piece formed a large puzzle that constantly worked together. According to Sam, we were only able to see the individual pieces, but when the Headmaster looked at it, he saw the whole puzzle. I found this point most interesting because it seemed to explain why we always try to piece things together, and why after thinking we've finally done it, we inevitably find another piece.

The farther we went, the more interesting the sights became, and the less I tried to make sense of it all or think about my apartment. My current surroundings had affected me in strange ways. I was surprised to find myself oblivious to the time and I began to billow with questions but tried to suppress my desire for answers. Every time I was about to speak, I stopped myself short and tried to pin point whether or not the question would make me seem greater or less than the man I'd been working hard to portray.

I could tell by the way Sam asked and answered questions that he didn't share my ambition to maintain his stature. It was as though he was oblivious to the way I perceived him. I was tempted to identify the attribute as utter naivety, but he carried an authority that could only be held by someone with supreme confidence. Naivety can be an insecurity that hinders people from truly engaging their minds to their environment. This leads them to become trapped by their desire not to know. Sam hadn't been afraid to interact on any of the topics that had drifted into our encounter and he certainly wasn't trapped. He sometimes asked very simple questions, but it was always because he sincerely wanted to know the answer. My act was beginning to tire me out.

While this was happening I was also fighting an internal battle, which was continually wearing me down. It was as though my heart had paid a visit to my brain, and the two were wrestling over which one had the better advice. The idea was slowly beginning to creep into my mind that there in fact might be a Headmaster, and that Sam really did work for him. I wasn't sure what had finally pushed me to contemplate the possibility that he was exactly who he said he was, but once the seed was planted, it started to grow. Some things still didn't add up though but I couldn't quite put my finger on what those things might be.

When we came over a hill, we could see what looked like huge streaks of gray, brown, and white running horizontally across the horizon. The colors hadn't been applied very smoothly and they formed a jagged messy streak. I thought that when we got closer I would see more clearly what the streaks actually were, but as we walked, they barely seemed to change and had become our permanent background. They stretched from the top of the horizon to past the clouds. The sight was more like an illusion than something in the real world. All of the things I had seen that seemed strange at first didn't compare to the unique quality of the colored streak. If the other items in the landscape formed one cohesive bond with each other, the streak at first seemed to be all on its own, not sure whether it was forming a bond with the land or the sky. But the more I looked, the more it seemed to be part of both worlds equally. It wasn't something I'd ever be used to looking at, and its presence was majestic.

The sky had changed color from a light blue to a darker blue and little white clouds dotted the expanse. Sam started to move more quickly and I could sense his excitement. I was surprised to see an abundance of water running freely across the ground in front of us. The water flowed under a wooden structure and wisped strands, small towers, and circles between its banks .

"Do you see that, Sam?" I asked with concern. "Maybe a large pipes burst. Look over there."

I pointed in the direction of the clear flowing liquid. Sam didn't seem to care about the waste and continued walking toward its banks.

"We should tell someone. They're going to run out at the building if this keeps up."

I wasn't sure where the concern had originated, but I started to get worried about the people in the building and wondered how they would cope if the water it produced was gone. I knew it was a real problem to run out of water because it was one of the only substances in the building that didn't seem to be counterfeit. Its importance was perceptible without having to put much effort into the act of perceiving. Sometimes, after a long day of trying to avoid the rotten air, or the people in the building, I would feel worn out. When I turned on the tap, I'd catch myself staring at the miraculous element, subdued by its intrigue.

Sam had a grin on his face as we reached the edge of the bank. We watched the wide body of water as it whipped up speed, gurgling and twisting around itself as it whizzed past.

"Do you want to jump in? The water's warm," said Sam with a smile.

It bothered me that Sam wasn't the least bit concerned about the problem we had discovered. He must have sensed my disgust and continued.

"It's OK, John. This water doesn't come from the building—it flows to it."

I didn't understand what Sam was trying to explain. I stared at the water as it raced along. The constant flow made me bubble with questions.

"If it doesn't come from the building, then why did they put it here? It seems a bit strange to produce the water so far from where the people use it. Is it a hazard to have it closer to the building?"

He stood close beside me and we watched a large tower float effortlessly over the surface of the water. It would have been very heavy because of its size, but it moved gently along the passageway as though it weighed nothing.

The image of the tower being carried over the water, combined with the talk of the Headmaster, had overcome my boundaries and I suddenly thought of my old colleague, Henry. He was one of the only people at the faculty who had become my friend. We were an unlikely pair. Although our personalities seemed to have clashed, we formed a connection not unlike the tower and the water. Like Sam, Henry also believed in the supernatural, but he rarely spoke of it. I took his belief to be a slight academic hiccup and was sure that I had a few of them myself.

We both had very different tastes when it came to ideas, women, and even clothing, but our bond was constant and at times we seemed to carry one another along. Our roles would switch back and forth. When the pressure of teaching courses became heavy on Henry, I would become the water, so to speak, and gently carry him along. In return, he would do the same for me when I was struggling to complete a paper. Our friendship was rarely threatened by outsiders because by all appearances, we seemed too different to get along so well, so the people around us never tried to meddle in the relationship. There were other people at the faculty who held more prestigious positions than the both of us combined, but their friendship came at a cost, along with an endless competition between others to be liked by them. Henry and I had managed to stay under the radar and wallow in our ambitions and failures while remaining unnoticed.

I don't know exactly why we had lost touch, but I had learned to push the memories aside. I can't put all of the blame on Henry, but he certainly wasn't the innocent one either. I had been rising in the ranks by producing high-quality papers. As my reputation grew, I had to feed it by attending events and making speeches at other universities. I expected Henry to recognize my accomplishments and thought our friendship would evolve. I was still planning to spend time with him, but thought he would understand why I couldn't engage in the same level of banter that I used to. I soon began to realize that he wasn't going to recognize my superior talent. I assumed he was angry with me for making more out of my career than he could and I stopped returning his calls.

When I had lost my position at the faculty, he tried to come for a visit, but I always delayed the invitations. I had reflected on the loss of our friendship once or twice over the months that followed, but the consuming power of dread that came with the memories forced me to abandon the entire relationship.

Sam and I stood together quietly and watched the tower finally disappear in the distance. I know Henry would have enjoyed watching the sight as much as I had.

Sam couldn't have known what I was thinking, but when the tower had vanished, he looked at me and it was as though his eyes had penetrated my soul. The sorrow had returned to his face and we both remained silent. After a few moments passed, he said, "The water doesn't get produced as though it were made in a factory."

"I don't know where they make it," I said. It should have been obvious to Sam from my tone that I wasn't an expert on the topic. "But it can't just appear out of nowhere, can it?" I finished my statement sarcastically.

"True enough, John," said Sam. "Let's just worry about getting across it for now."

My concern must have been shallower than my outburst warranted because his suggestion to continue our study quickly squashed my distress.

After a few moments he nodded toward the wooden structure that crossed the water and we began walking toward it.

"What do you think of the puzzle, John? Have you seen enough for today?"

The more time we spent walking together, the more I liked Sam. Maybe he had strange ideas about how things are, but so did Henry. Of course Henry didn't care if I believed them. I couldn't put my finger on Sam's motives, but he had a kind way about him and there wasn't a hint of mischief in his bones. I didn't realize how much I'd missed the company of another human being until this afternoon. Even when I disliked people, I still had never preferred being alone. I wasn't sure why I'd stopped reaching out to other people, but if I'd learned anything of substance today, it was to rekindle some of my old friendships. I had too much on my mind and didn't want to go back to my apartment. I was hoping that Sam wasn't trying to send me away.

"Almost, Sam, but I could see some more," I replied.

"That's what I was hoping," he remarked. "Come with me."

10

WE WALKED ACROSS THE wooden connection and when we arrived at the other side, Sam started to make his way up a steep hill to the left. It took some effort to climb and when we reached the top, we stood on a large platform that overlooked the valley we had just come from. The green wigs looked like large patches of mismatched spots, and most of the colorful circles were covered. We walked to the edge of the platform where there was a railing with two white telescopes attached to it. Sam led the way and waved for me to follow. He reached the telescopes first and signaled for me to use the one on the left before peering into the one on the right.

"You feel at home now don't you, John," he mumbled as he moved his lens back and forth.

It seemed like the telescopes were pointed in a rather odd direction, but I wasn't going to complain about the opportunity to use one. I grabbed hold of the top of the telescope and pulled it down to make it level with my eyes. I squinted my left eye carefully, settled my feet into place, and peered through the tiny glass window. The lens shot a wide angle view of the valley.

"There's something wrong with this one," I said with a proud voice. "It's the focus, or the lens."

"Mine seems to work perfectly," replied Sam with glee.

I tried to adjust the lens.

"No, there's still something wrong. It may have gotten wet inside," I said.

Sam kept one eye buried in the telescope and looked up at me with the other one. "Slow down, John, look closely."

I felt discouraged and looked away from the lens for a moment. I squinted my eyes and again peered through.

"It must be broken. I can barely see the wigs and there's a mix of colors bouncing around. I see lines and shapes that aren't supposed to be there. There's more than just water on the lens. Whoa!" I exclaimed. "Did you see that?"

I jumped back from the telescope, my heart beating quickly. Sam didn't move at all.

"What did you see, John?" he asked.

"It was like a flare up, or maybe a cosmic spray. . . . Er, I don't know. . . ."

I did my best to regain my orientation, but felt as though I'd been transported to another galaxy.

"Look again, John, it's wonderful."

I walked back toward the telescope and looked through the lens. The lines were still there and the colors bounced around.

"I saw it again," I said with laughter in my voice.

"See, nothing to be scared of. Awe is not the same as fear."

I was glued to the lens. My heart rate stayed high and my hands were beginning to sweat.

At first it looked as though a partially transparent blue grid covered the entire landscape, like a blanket over a bed. The lines that made up the grid were very fine, and followed the contour of the area, making the land look as though it were perfectly proportioned. As I looked on, I began to see that there was another grid in the color orange, this one made up of triangles. At first it looked as though the triangles were flat, parallel to the blue grid, but I also noticed that they seemed to protrude into the air, depending on which direction I looked through the telescope. From this perspective, they seemed to be above the ground, their points reaching into the heavens. It was as though the landscape were more of an Escher painting, than that of a Hopper. After that, I noticed thousands upon thousands of circles, all chained together, and in a myriad of colors, each swirling and spinning, as though a great delicate necklace of enormous stature had been loosely dropped from above. The startling difference between the circles and the other two shapes was that rather than being nearly translucent, but otherwise complete, the circles were more like giant rings of fire, obviously in the shape of a circle, but not steadfast in their form. And every once in a while, the tops of some of the circles would dart into the air, as though flames were shooting up fast like a bullet, before disappearing out of sight.

For the first time since I could remember, I let go of every thought I'd been holding on to, even the ones that had been there for years. My mind was going completely blank and I had nowhere else to be. It's the type of moment that's best described when it's over. While it's happening you wouldn't want to waste your time describing it, and a certain part of you is shouting that somehow it will never leave anyways. It's the type of moment that speaks its own language and whispers beautiful words in your ear. You could never pin point when it started, or know exactly when it ended, but while you were in it, it felt like the only moment you'd ever had, or ever needed to have. My brain told me that as long as I was looking through the telescope, I would stay where I was forever, and so we continued to look at the beautiful landscape, not saying a word. It was the best type of moment. The kind that's perfect for what it is and at the same time promises that when it's over, it will come back again someday. A moment that can be described justly by only one short word—joy.

I noticed Sam looking in my direction from the corner of my eye several times as we stared through our lenses. He was watching me closely, but was careful not to speak even though I could sense his enjoyment from where I was standing.

For some reason I couldn't get the thought of Henry out of mind, even after seeing what I'd just seen. When we finally faced each other on the platform, Sam acted cautiously. It was as though he was handling something delicate and he didn't want it to break.

"It's going to be dark soon, John. Let's say good bye to the valley and head back to the elevator," he spoke calmly.

11

OUR RAPID PACE FROM earlier in the day had slowed considerably and we sauntered like old friends toward the edge of the platform.

"It never gets old," Sam remarked as we made our descent back to the valley floor. The terrain was steep, but our feet were heavy and we lumbered along, going down the hill with ease. We were both lost in our own minds, deep in thought, and happy about it.

"What was that?" I finally asked as we neared the stream.

The sky was made up of several shades of blue now, with the farthest point being the darkest. The sun was nearing the painted streaks of gray and I watched it closely to see what would happen when the two met in the sky.

"There are two parts to this world, John."

"Yes I know, two different clocks," I said.

"No, not that. I mean two different aspects to the actual world."

"What do you mean?" I asked, as we walked over the wooden bridge side by side.

"There are the things that humans can see with the naked eye, and there are the things humans can't see."

"OK, I think I see what you mean," I said. "What were we looking at back there? Were those some kind of tiny atoms?"

"We would include anything that can been seen through a microscope to be an extension of the naked eye."

The water gurgled as it rippled under the wooden walkway. Our steps made a loud hollow bang each time they landed on the finely cut surface.

"Then what were we looking at?" I asked.

"All of things that can't be seen with the naked eye," Sam replied as though it was an obvious answer.

"There are many aspects to the world that are not visible, but just because you can't see them doesn't mean they don't exist. Nothing is completely hidden and so people are free to discover what's there through other means, using mathematical equations, models, art, philosophy, and experience. The telescopes gave us a glimpse into some of those things.

"If you can't see something, then can you really be sure that it's there? Even if you can model it through math, the math could change once a new formula is discovered," I stated.

"There are certain things people can prove, and certain things that they take on faith," said Sam. "Some things are easy to prove, for example, the fact that you're taller than me. Other things are more difficult. Then there are things like gravity. We can't see it, but we have pretty good observational data to support that it is there, and no one is afraid that when they wake up in the morning they might suddenly float away. We take it on faith that gravity exists and not only that, we believe it's unchanging. Morality, justice, pleasure, and wisdom are similar. Right won't suddenly become wrong, and wrong suddenly right. We know, without being able to prove the idea with evidence, that there's order to everything. Most people believe that murder is immoral and that murder will stay immoral. Attributes like envy, jealousy, and greed are similar."

I thought most of what Sam said was right, but didn't believe all of it, and tried to poke a hole in his logic.

"I think I understand what you mean. It's like trying to figure out how the universe came to exist. We have to take it on faith that it just came into being at some point."

"That's not entirely true, John. Rational thinking can show how the universe began to exist."

"Sure, in a sense. We can infer the hypothesis based on what we observe, that we all came from particles which evolved over time, but we don't ultimately know how that first moment began. Think about it, Sam. There was no space, no time, no material, just

nothing, and then suddenly there was something. It's the defini-
tion of faith."

"You're partly right, but since nothing can come from nothing, there must have been a cause of space, time, and the material
universe. Otherwise, you're left with irrationality. That's where the
Headmaster comes in."

I knew this was a trick. Sam couldn't get this one past me.

"That's not fair—this is why I study science. It's the ultimate,
most honorable way of finding answers to life's most difficult questions. You can't just say the Headmaster did it, and think you've
found the answer."

"You prove my own point, John. Come, let's sit down for a
moment."

We had made it over the current and sat down beside each
other on a lonely fallen tower that was resting just off of the bank
of the stream. Sam crossed his legs and looked at the water. Its
swish was as endless as the stars on a flawlessly clear night.

"Having a creative source is the only way that the universe
makes sense. You can't say that everything came from a bunch of
random particles, and then in the next breathe say it's honorable
and worth exploring. That's irrational—like calling something a
square circle."

"I think you're being naive, Sam," I finally replied. "How can
you think that all of the discoveries we've made came from anything other than human ingenuity? To just say the Headmaster did
it is a cop out, and that line of thinking will make people lazy and
stop discovering, which will hamper progress. Show me how the
universe can be explained without science. Show me something
beyond nature. If you can do that, I'll walk down whatever road
you want."

"Try breaking it down, John. How could anything at all begin
to exist without a cause?"

"What do you mean?" I replied.

"If things randomly popped into existence, why aren't we
worried that a lion will suddenly appear and eat us for dinner. And

if everything needs a cause to exist, and the universe exists, then it follows that the universe must have had a cause, doesn't it?"

"So, there's a hole in the logic. That doesn't mean we can't fill it in the future."

"There will never be such a thing as a square circle."

Sam paused for a moment and then said, "You know, mankind's curiosity can be both its best ally and its worst enemy. It's submission, John."

"What's submission?"

"Do you see the error? It's clear to me, but for those who are making it, it's like a black hole, an endless abyss. Curiosity has a slight tendency to extol itself, by quickly replacing the act of discovering with that of creation. It's easy to see how it happens. Prideful consciousness is like a megaphone and discovery is like a platform. Your specific occupation is prone to this sort of thing, but everyone's susceptible to it in varying degrees. Philosophers create all sorts of realities, even suggesting we're just a brain in a vat, but even children know that can't be true. People will do anything to acknowledge themselves over the Headmaster because prideful consciousness is powerful. People think that if they submit, then they won't be heard. But they don't stop to remember that they don't have to worry, because he hears everything."

The air was beginning to cool slightly and I realized that I hadn't been thinking about germs for some time, or my apartment, or any of my former colleagues. When I took a gulp of the invisible substance, I noticed that it had changed its taste just slightly and it soothed my throat as I took in each breath. I was thinking about what Sam had said when I starting hearing sounds all around me. The more I listened, the louder they became, and it felt as though an orchestra was blasting in our ears. The groans and creaks snapped with intensity and broke the calm atmosphere. I looked at Sam and shouted, "Don't you hear that?"

"You don't have to shout, they're just crickets," he replied pleasantly.

I could hear his voice perfectly normally and the sound of the creatures faded into the background.

"They must be everywhere," I remarked, as I tried to spot one. Suddenly, a small black creature landed on my leg. Its antenna stuck up from its head and its legs looked so delicate that I thought they might bend under the weight of its body. It looked around, its head moving rapidly back and forth with obvious intent. I wondered if it was doing the same thing as me—investigating the foreign life form that sat comfortably on its favorite tower. Did it know more about the world than I do? Could it see the things we looked at through the telescope without using an assisting device? Maybe size was the real error of perception. I was larger than this little guy, just as the planets are larger than me, but that doesn't mean its faculties couldn't be far more superior.

When the cricket moved from place to place on my lap, it did so in small successive leaps, slowly turning its entire body 15 degrees at a time until it was finally facing the other way. I looked closely and could see its beady round eyes staring back at mine. It was a complex creature and very fine indeed. I thought about what Sam had said while I enjoyed a moment with the creature.

"You just can't face a purposeless existence, Sam," I finally asserted.

"Your ideas shoot themselves in the head, John. Aside from the fact that you can't get something from nothing, if we all came from a meaningless bunch of atoms, bouncing through space, then everything you've just explained is also meaningless. How can your thoughts be trusted if at the bottom, you're part of a mindless process of evolving particles—cold and uncaring—until the heat death of the universe destroys everything? When left on its own, all science can show is that science itself is dead."

I felt angry, and subdued.

"We find it honorable and worthwhile to investigate nature, and even things like morality and justice, because it's more than just particles evolving, and therefore, worth being called wonderful. Without the Headmaster, the term 'worthwhile' wouldn't even be a term. If the universe is meaningless, so is worth. You can't surmise about a thing that isn't real, but you can guess wrongly about a thing that is. You might see a car and think it's a Chevrolet when it's actually a Ford, but you wouldn't say anything if there were no car. What I mean is, if you say the universe is at its root purposeless, then there is no such thing as worth, morality, wisdom, or justice. You might think that morality comes from nature itself, but that's because you've just attributed its origin to the wrong cause."

Sam's voice boomed as he ended his sentence, but I could tell that his tone wasn't driven by anger. I wanted to defend my position, but I wasn't sure how.

"You're trying to confuse me, Sam. I know nature does something to us, even if it can't stand on its own. And that's the real reason I became I scientist."

"As they say, John, you can't have your cake and eat it too. The amenities certainly have the ability to stun us when we consider them carefully, and so they should."

Sam thought to himself for a moment.

"I've also been showing you something far more powerful than everything we've discussed, and seen since we met this morning. The amenities are beyond us, and there are many attributes beyond them, but we've also been given the ability not just to witness, but to wield the greatest power of them all, and that's love. It's also the most damaging power to flip, far worse than flipping time."

The cricket leapt from my leg and was once again lost in the sea of blades. I felt a dull pain when he disappeared, as though I had made a friend and then lost one, all within a couple of minutes.

"You're not my toughest case, but you're not my easiest either," said Sam with an empathetic voice. "We usually wait until you've started using the amenities again, but I'd like to show you one more thing before the evening is over."

I had neared the end of my wits, and suddenly felt uncomfortable with the dialogue.

"I'm getting a little tired, Sam, how much farther are we going to have to go?"

"You should take off those weights, John, they've been slowing you down since we met."

"Weights?"

"Yes, John, the weights. Don't you remember? You put them on years ago. You were doing an experiment to disprove one of Einstein's equations. You showed a hypothesis to one of your colleagues and he said you could never prove it. The weights are strapped to your legs and around your chest. Look under your clothes."

I was scared to acknowledge what Sam had said. He was right about the sunglasses, could he be right about this too? I grabbed the bottom of one pant leg and pulled it up, slowly revealing a black strap with two large bulges, one on the front and one on the back, wrapped tightly around my leg. The back strap remained tight due to some Velcro and I pulled it away from itself, dislodging the object from my ankle. It felt heavy in my hands. The skin underneath was bare and smooth. I pulled up my other pant leg and saw a similar object. After removing the second one, I stood and faced Sam, who was still perched on the fallen tower. He must have sensed my shame because he reached out his hand and patted me on the back of my ankle.

"It's alright, John, I'm glad to be the one who pointed it out. Sometimes ideas seem right at the time, but it often takes a friend to correct them."

I couldn't remember putting the weights on my body, but after looking at my legs, I could tell that they had been there for a long time. I lifted my shirt and saw that I had on what looked like a sleek backpack. It was black and snug to my body. I pulled the wide Velcro strap at the front of the bag and pulled my arms through the shoulder straps. I let the bag slip from my body and it made a dull thud as it hit the ground. The tightness that had plagued my torso was gone in an instant and my shoulders felt as though they had lifted four inches. I bent my neck back and forth and breathed a sigh of relief. The whole world seemed to get lighter and all of my limbs felt like jello.

"Why was I wearing those, Sam? What possessed me to . . ." I stopped talking mid-sentence. I couldn't help but reflect on all those wasted years of aches and pains that I'd caused to my own body.

"I'm a reasonable person, Sam. . . . I didn't know, er, it must have been smart at the time and I'd become used to wearing them," I tried to explain.

"I'm sure it was, but it was time to move on. Time doesn't make a poor decision better, but it's never too late to admit a mistake and stop making it. You're free from the weights now. Try not to think about it and enjoy your new freedom."

Sam possessed a surety in his tone that made me want to believe him. He stood from the log and took the weights in his hand.

"I'll put these in the exercise room at the building."

12

WE BEGAN TO RETRACE our steps and head back to the elevator. The sun was almost out of sight by the time we reached it and the sky was fading from blue to black. Along the way I noticed even more creatures than we had when we first walked through the open space, and was especially surprised at how many of them knew how to fly. Sam hit the down button and the doors opened after sounding their familiar chime. Once inside, Sam pressed the D button and we slowly began our descent.

My mind was racing and my limbs had never felt better. My whole body was loose and I had the freedom to move my arms and legs without the fear of inevitable pain. I had told Sam I was tired, but that wasn't exactly true. Having your ideas stripped can bring you to a state of vulnerability that you know might be for the better, but which feels rather prickly at the time. He had certainly worn me down, but the tiredness was more like the feeling you get when you've worked hard at something, as opposed to that of laziness. I felt like a child again for a couple of brief moments, and the sensation brought with it long-past memories that were now more like feelings that actual events. They were warm, fleeting, and impossible to grasp. We stood quietly in the elevator when suddenly the tea came to my mind again.

"When will it wear off, Sam, the tea I mean?" I asked.

I had come to respect Sam and asked the question bluntly, sure that he would give me a straight answer this time.

"The tea?" he asked with an innocent voice.

I felt a sharp sense of embarrassment for seeming paranoid, but I couldn't think of how else to explain what had been happening over the course of the day. I couldn't have been so blind to my surroundings. I'd been considering the option that indeed there was a road, and that I'd somehow lost my way, since we walked away from the telescopes, but that was impossible. I was John, the one who had defined time. How could I have invented most of what I thought was real and lost sight of so much beauty?

"There must have been something in that tea. I've been seeing radical things all day and I certainly don't feel like myself. It's not exactly a woozy feeling, but something is different. I've been having deep moments of . . . calm."

I looked over at Sam who was looking straight ahead. His brow was furrowed. He looked like he was busy in his own mind, but also listening intently.

"It's not the tea, John."

The elevator chimed not long after the doors had closed, indicating that we had come to a halt at our desired level. When we walked out the night sky had almost completely engulfed what was once a bright sunny day. Tiny white lights sparkled as an umbrella inviting us to walk under their cover. The moon was in the distance, casting a dull illumination that far surpassed the intensity of any artificial light source, but was easy on the eyes. Its deep craters were visible without the help of any device and the thought of equations jumped through my mind momentarily. When the stars lost their hold on my attention, I scanned our environment and began to recognize some of the features on level D. We were walking down a stone pathway that felt very familiar and it led toward a large fountain. Brown towers lined the edges of the walkway with several benches scattered between them along the way. In the distance, I could see a children's play area adorned with a swing set, slides, and teeter-totter. Memories began to clash with the calm sensation I'd been feeling. It seemed as though the self I'd known was taking over again, but that the new knowledge, which I'd been collecting over the day, was trying to hold its position.

I must have been too engaged by the new sights to notice at first, but now I saw that all kinds of people were sprinkled around us. Some walked quickly past while other sat on the benches. The more I looked, the more people I saw, as if Sam had invited everyone in the building to enjoy the night sky with us. Just then a group of children ran past with their mother and father following close behind. One of them bumped my leg, slowing him down, but without hesitation he picked up speed and continued his journey.

"Oh, we're so sorry," said the boy's mother as she put her hand on my shoulder. "Slow down!" she exclaimed in a merry voice.

I flinched when she touched me and involuntarily stepped a couple of feet away from her. She continued walking as though she hadn't noticed my reaction.

"I've been here before," I observed to Sam. "Where are we now?"

"Of course you have, John. We're at the park across the street from the building,"

When we reached the fountain, Sam stopped to take a look. We watched the large concrete sculpture replenish itself by pulling the water from its pool and spewing it back out of its top. A group of young people sat on the edge of the fountain. They were talking loudly and they used exaggerated gestures when they spoke. As I watched the youth in their banter, I couldn't help but remember how it was to be young, and paused to reflect.

There was an exuberance in the air, as though everything was before them, and I could remember having that same aura. I thought about what Sam had said about being the same person now as I was back then. Was it true that my fledgling characteristics were still intact? The whole atmosphere seemed to contribute to this moment of nostalgia. I could suddenly smell the air again and felt comforted by the speckled blanket that covered us. A muffled sound of voices held their ground against the sound of the breeze that ruffled the hairs on the wigs atop the brown towers. I felt a strong urge to insert myself into the center of a group and submerge myself into the talk of the day. The instinct came and went with a forceful push as I dared myself on, but I let the ambition fade into the night sky.

"Why are all of these people out tonight?" I asked.

"They're out here every night," said Sam.

"I don't ever remember seeing them, even when I do leave the apartment."

"When the power of love gets flipped on itself, almost everyone and everything disappears. Love is outward, not inward, and consciousness is only useful when it's not focused on itself."

The sight of the people and movement of sound waves had finally pushed all thought out of my head. I forgot about the faculty, my work, my career, and even Sam's motives.

It's a feeling I had longed to experience, because I could remember distinctly that at some point in my life I had no cares in the world. It had been so long since my mind was totally blank that as I got older, I started to think that I'd created the idea that my mind really ever had been blank. I thought it might be wishful thinking, and that although I was sure it had happened to me frequently as a child, I must have actually invented that state of mind. The exertion expounded by trying not to think was so great that the effort only caused me to hold onto my identity even tighter. So I had stopped trying to try, many years ago. I somehow thought that if I didn't uphold my own desires, I would become nothing, as though I would suddenly vanish. Clinging to myself is what gave me purpose.

It was as though Sam's thoughts and mine were somehow synchronized, because as soon as my mind was completely blank, he declared that we had spent enough time at the fountain and that we would reach our destination very soon.

I followed closely behind Sam as he guided us down the pathway. When we reached the end I was dizzy from all of the bodies that had moved past us. The area was busy with people of all ages, and the interaction, though from a distance, had affected me.

"We're here," said Sam.

The path had led directly to a road. There was a sign pointing to the east that read, "Dead End." I looked down the road in the direction of the sign and saw that it led directly to the building. The other sign pointed to the west and read, "The Way." When I looked in that direction, I saw that the road was visible for a short distance, and then took a sharp right turn, making any further observation impossible. I could see a few people walking down the road toward us as though they were heading back to the building.

"I think I know where we are. But why are those people heading back toward the old building, don't people go to the new building at night?" I asked.

"People don't travel the road much at night. The day is the best time," said Sam. "And the building isn't ready yet."

"Right. If the building isn't there yet, what's the point of going on a road that leads to nowhere?" I asked.

"We always get the same response." said Sam. The sorrow that had left his voice for most of the day had returned. He looked at me with his sharp eyes.

"You used to run up and down the road when you were a boy, don't you remember, John?"

"We would send you maps in the mail. Your mother used to tell you the way, but we also wanted you to know how to get there on your own. She would give you the maps that we had sent and you would make a game out of going as far down the road as you could. She was always thrilled at your progress."

Sam seemed to drift a little as he spoke, as though he wasn't sure if I was really listening. I couldn't remember the events that Sam was telling me about, but I reveled in the thought of being a child again. The word "child" reminded me of the word "innocence" and every time I heard it, the word seemed to wash my mind, as though it were sprinkled with water, if only for an instant.

"Tell me when the new building will be finished and I'll know when to pack my things." It seemed like a reasonable demand, and one that would satisfy the lingering question of Sam's intentions.

"We've been telling you for years now. Through signs, maps, and letters, or what you might call logic, reason, and conscience. Your own father and mother explained it a thousand times."

"Why don't I remember?" I asked.

"The less time you spend on the road, the more distracted from it you become. The building has brilliant amenities, nothing more so than the stars, but like consciousness, they're not a means to their own end. When the thought of discovering life is replaced by ownership, then pride becomes your one true master. The stars are brilliant, though. Can you tell me what they're made up of?" asked Sam with a curious voice.

I was glad that Sam had asked the question. I had felt like a student for the last few hours and it was competing with my tendency to be heard rather than to listen.

"It's pretty complex, Sam." I said.

I hoped I didn't sound to demeaning and that Sam would continue listening. He nodded, indicating for me to continue.

"They're essentially big balls of gas, mostly hydrogen and helium, and they're constantly undergoing a sort of nuclear reaction." I was proud that I could formulate a simple answer so quickly.

"Big balls of hydrogen and helium?" asked Sam.

"Yes, that's right." It made me happy for Sam to reiterate my knowledge.

"I wonder how you would view the stars if your perception of time had been flipped all of these years?"

"What do you mean?" I asked.

"John, when time is a countdown, you perceive everything differently, not just the stars. It's like when you go on a long-deserved vacation to the cottage, but only for a few short days. When you know you won't be there long, the cottage transforms into a palace, not just wooden studs. The lake becomes the place where your cares are relinquished. It becomes your psychiatrist, and not just a body of water. Every little utensil and every magazine on every nook and counter is your intimate companion. You have a deep appreciation for everything, but without holding onto anything too tight, because the reason it rejuvenates you is due to the fact that it won't last very long. An urgency mixes with delicacy, mixes with awe, and you begin to see things not just as objects, but as parts of a larger picture, and far more profound. When time is counting down, all of life becomes this way, especially the other people. You can be completely captivated, but at the same time, able and willing to let go, knowing that the thing itself is not the whole point."

I saw what he was trying to do and maybe he had a point. Had I given up my life for hydrogen and helium, and missed the bigger picture? Maybe I'd been so busy looking for something new, or if I'm honest, looking to be acknowledged by finding the things I was looking for, that I'd read the signs completely wrong.

"You sound like one of those anti-scientists. I'm used to dealing with guys like you. They spend their time researching why people like me are wrong instead of making their own discoveries."

"Unfortunately, I know the type," replied Sam.

He rested his arm on my back and smiled wide, as though we shared a common camaraderie that was pulling us closer together.

"A lot of those folks are also distracted from the road. Just as you've been distracted by the stars, they've been distracted by proving others wrong."

"Wouldn't you want the people on the road to prove a guy like me wrong?" I asked.

Some of the people who had been walking toward us were now getting very close to where Sam and I stood. I wasn't sure what to expect when they passed and I clenched my hand tightly, as though I was bracing for something.

"That depends on their motives," Sam replied. "The people on the road have two ultimate purposes."

"What are those?" I asked.

"To help people get back on the road, and to help those who are on it from being distracted away from it."

Just then the young lady who I had been observing walked past where we were standing. I watched her closely to see if anything was different about her, but noticed nothing in particular. She glanced up just as she passed where we stood and her eyes twinkled. Sam leaned his back against a post near where the edge of the sidewalk transitioned onto the smooth surface of the road. He crossed his right leg over his left leg and stood tall, in a comfortable position.

It had been a long day for both of us, but Sam had been nothing but kind toward me, spending much of his energy encouraging me to continue. At the time, I thought he was trying to get something from me, because I couldn't understand why someone would want good for another fellow, unless they wanted something in return. As the day progressed, Sam had shown me many great things, and although I continued to expect his demand for reciprocation, it never came. He seemed to take pleasure in giving, and when he sensed that something was amiss, he quickly reassured me with intense sincerity. I began to conclude that Sam considered my well-being to be superior to his, and I could see that he gained immense satisfaction from this orientation. He didn't seem to want anything and it struck me as odd.

I took the moment to have a closer look at my companion. Even after having spent so many hours together, I had never really taken in most of his features, other than to notice that he wasn't much older than me, and that his hair had turned from gray to blonde after I had taken off my sunglasses. Sam seemed to be off somewhere, drifting in his own mind, and had the look of someone who is utterly content to just be.

I didn't want him to notice me looking at him so I purposely stood a pace behind where his feet were planted and a couple of feet to his right. I scanned my eyes across the ground and then quickly lifted them toward his face for a brief moment, before looking over his head and back down the road. Sam didn't seem to want to move and I continued the maneuver, looking over his face several times. After considering his features, my only perception of him that had changed from the idea that I had been carrying in my mind was that he had a twinkle in his eye, similar to that of the woman who had passed us. On all other accounts he seemed to be a regular person.

As I reflected on the events of the day I recognized that the things I thought I knew were true seemed to be vanishing from my skull, like when a strong storm hits the port unannounced and carries the old wooden schooners out to sea without a trace. As my thoughts left, I was scared that they wouldn't be replaced by anything else, and that all I'd be left with after spending the day with Sam was a hollowed-out brain. I couldn't tell now whether I was relieved or panicked to be stripped in this way. My back felt better though, and so did my legs. I also reveled in the colors.

Suddenly, an indescribable urge came over me. It was as though a wave had been chasing me all day and had finally crashed on my head.

"I want to keep going!" I exclaimed, breaking the silence.

Sam turned his face toward me and a small smile started to appear as he looked at me. His eyes seemed to twinkle a little brighter than before and I was anxious for him to respond.

"I know we shouldn't go too far at night, but I'd like to have a look."

I tried to cover up my excitement, but I don't think I was very successful. Sam didn't move from his slanted position and waved me forward with his hand without taking his eyes off of mine. I stepped down from the sidewalk and onto the road. Several street-lights lined my passageway with their bright bulbs glaring down upon the paved surface.

I began to walk, slowly at first, being careful to understand my surroundings. Another one of the people whom I had seen earlier walked past me now. I was careful not to look too closely, but noticed the same twinkle in his eye as in the woman's. My anticipation began to grow as I reached the corner that had inhibited any further inspection from my previous position. As I rounded it, I was surprised to see that the road abruptly ended. After the turn there was only 40 feet of road, and it ended at a large wooden door.

On the left and right side of the road there were only green blades and brown towers. The door was as wide as the road and I could see that it was the entrance to a structure, and that the structure wasn't much taller or wider than the door itself. I didn't know how far back the building went, but based on the size of the door, I thought it had to be an impressive size. I looked back toward Sam and saw that he was no longer leaning on the post. When I looked ahead again he was standing right in front of me, chewing a small piece of one of the green blades. I fell to the ground in disbelief. Sam's look changed from merriment to concern and he quickly helped me back to my feet.

"Are you OK, John?" he asked.

I wiped the dust and pebbles from my pant legs, somewhat unsurprised at his stunt, and yet unable to speak for a moment. Sam saw me struggling to talk and gave me a solid pat on the back. I stopped trying to form words and let my nerves calm.

"I didn't expect the road to end here," I finally said.

"How would you know, John? You haven't been here since you were born."

"Born? You said I came here as a boy." I was perplexed at Sam's remark.

"You were on the road as a boy," Sam replied, "I wouldn't expect you to remember being here though."

"Where are we?" I asked.

"That door leads to the Headmaster's son. He's who you speak to about getting back on the road. Everyone's been here at some point in their life, and some knock without ever getting all of the way off the road, while others knock only once they've been off. The point is, in order to stay on the road, or get back on, everyone has to knock."

My anticipation was suddenly replaced by a sense of confusion. The night sky continued to sparkle with the bright speckles of the stars. From where we stood, I could still see the moon clearly and the deep ancient craters shouted of their magnificence. It hovered in the air like a giant button that was pinned in place to a seemingly flat background. Sam stood quietly beside me as we stared at the door together. A slight breeze passed us by and shook the green wigs of the brown towers. The wigs made the sound of water rushing over rocks as the air lifted and pushed them. The movement was free and fluid, and the wigs revealed the direction of the invisible force. It made me think that the only predictability of wind is that it doesn't follow any rules.

"If this isn't the road, then where is it?" I said.

"The road isn't physical, John," he replied.

The wind continued hustling past us lightly and the green wigs continued dancing. The sound had become calm and I noticed that Sam and I were alone together. A kind of force had been following Sam all day and I could sense its power every so often. At first I thought it was because he was very persuasive when he wanted something from somebody, but when I realized that there wasn't a devious bone in his body, I was at a loss for what it was. The draw was for another reason that I couldn't put my fingers on. It would pull hard in some moments and then let go quickly. Other times I felt only a hint of the sensation and I couldn't tell whether or not I'd imagined the instances of the force. My only other recognition of it came when I thought about Henry. I felt sure now that Sam possessed an unspeakable quality because its strength became relentless.

The atmosphere felt heavy and suddenly soaked me in itself. The weight was delightful, and although it pushed me down to the ground, the most comfortable position was to stand up straight and tall. I knew that the force wasn't coming from myself, but it so completely filled my insides that it had the illusion of being self-induced. I had learned from my earlier experiences with Sam that it was best not to try and hold the moment, but to let it be, because the force was going to do what it wanted.

Sam's arms were crossed and he looked comfortable. His demeanour told me that he still wasn't in a rush to get away and I wondered if he was enjoying this time as much as I was.

"I've never heard of a non-physical road," I said with suspicion.

"Of course you have, John. Haven't you ever heard someone say 'I've been down this road before,' when they describe having a baby or finding a new job." I understood Sam's point and didn't say anything.

"Not everything is physical, remember. Our knowledge of existence isn't physical, but we certainly know that we exist."

Just then, a small creature came darting out from the side of the structure. It scurried along the ground, its four feet moving quickly. When it reached the bottom of one of the brown towers, it stopped and looked toward us. I could see its eyes twinkle from the light of the moon. After a second or two, it defied the laws of gravity, and from a completely vertical position, shot itself up and disappeared into the green wigs. Its tail wiggled back and forth as it made its ascent.

"What was that?" I asked enthusiastically.

"Don't leave food lying around near those little ones," laughed Sam. "They'll practically snap it right out of your hands."

The sight of the creature had stirred my senses and I could feel the final traces of my guard slip right through my fingers. I no longer had the energy or the wits to defend myself from a psychological attack. I knew I was at a disadvantage, but I had no fear of Sam. It was as though I suddenly had no thoughts of my past and no expectations for the future.

"If we're talking about a metaphoric road, there's plenty to choose from. Why would I walk down your road?" I asked.

"The road is not a metaphor, it's a real road—you just can't see it. But when you're on it, you know it," said Sam. "In fact, being on the road is the only place where you know anything for sure and are completely free."

"All roads have constraints. It's the mother of invention."

"Not *the* road," said Sam. "If you're anywhere other than the road, you'll be subject to something. We were designed with a purpose, and when we bypass the way things are intended, our instincts continue to search for purpose as a natural inclination. You may look for it in your career, ambition, materials, people, pleasure, or even your dreams and desires. The people on the road are subject to none but him who built it, and he, by his nature, is beyond all rules and laws."

"Nothing is beyond all rules and laws," I replied. "Nature itself is subject to the laws of nature, and we're a part of nature. Never mind the laws of the land. Imagine the chaos if people didn't follow the law."

"It's because people aren't on the road that there needs to be law," said Sam. "And the Headmaster isn't limited by what he made, just as the man who carves a decoration from wood isn't suddenly destined to be an ornament on the mantel."

I began to feel slightly dizzy, but in the best sort of way. My heartbeat was picking up speed and my mind was rapidly crunching the information that Sam threw my way.

"How can people get onto a non-physical, invisible road?"

"You'll have to speak with the son. He'll want an explanation as to why you got off in the first place, because he will explain things to the Headmaster as though it were his fault you left, and take the blame for everything. He's a good friend that way, but only if you're honest about your reasons for getting off. The road was given as a free gift and we were all made to walk down it, so make sure you apologize. He'll let you back on. And don't bother lying to him—he knows."

"I didn't mean who do I speak with to get on the road, I mean how do I get to it? Let's say I speak with the son—where do I go from there?"

"You won't have to go anywhere," Sam said, "That's precisely what I've explained."

Sam seemed slightly frustrated for the first time since I met him. The sadness had returned to his voice momentarily. "You humans are lovable, but you sometimes lack listening skills."

Without warning, I started to feel a warmth running from the bottom of my toes and up toward the top of my head. It was as though the moon had suddenly taken on the discreet qualities of the sun. The sensation now became centralized in the middle of my chest. My heart started to beat a little quicker and with much more force. My attention was being drawn to its burning pulse. It felt as though I was returning home after a long trip. My mind dripped with the aura of memories, and although I kept trying, I couldn't picture any specific events. I longed for the moment to last, but knew that the longing was hindering the very thing I was yearning to hold. I tried to restrain myself from want and again focused on the rhythm of my heart.

The world around me suddenly became larger than it was before. The brown tower was far away and at the same time leaned right over me. I could feel the hardness of the stone road under my feet while I simultaneously floated above it. The wind was cool on my face and its touch warmed my insides as though a woman had put her hand on my cheek. The atmosphere that had been pushing me into the ground with its delightful force was holding me in place. I wanted to walk up to the door and start pounding. Part of me wanted to find out if everything Sam had said was in fact right, but the truth was I simply had no other urge than to knock, and could do nothing to control it. The door was only a few paces from where I stood.

Suddenly, I was struck by fear. What if the son wouldn't open the door when I knocked? If everything Sam had said was in fact true, then I had some explaining to do. If he was anything like me, he wouldn't accept a deserter, especially if he had to take the blame when I got off the road. It was the kind of fear that's so closely linked to excitement that I felt soothed.

Sam turned to me and a wide smile formed on his face, bringing with it a mesmerizing light in his twinkling eyes. He put his arm around my back for the final time. His hand clenched my shoulder. The moment suddenly began to move faster, although we stood perfectly still, and I couldn't suppress the longing for time to stop. I was acutely aware of the upper right side of my body where Sam's hand met my shoulder. The power of words, and the atmosphere they created, were no match for the power of Sam's touch.

"I have to get going now, John but don't rush," said Sam with a calm steady voice. "I'll be in the basement tomorrow if you'd like to drop by for a cup of tea."

In an instant, I was alone, as though Sam had disappeared into thin air. The door towered above my head and seemed to get taller the longer I looked at it. In the next moment, without even thinking, I made my hand into a first and drew it far behind my head.

❧

When I woke up, all I could hear was the sound of several large men laughing, their baritone chuckles almost like a long, soothing, gurgle. There were at least four different pitches, but I couldn't place them.

I felt disoriented and could barely move my body. When I finally tried to lift my head, I realized my face was stuck to a piece of paper that had been resting on a desk in front of me. The paper made a soft sticky sound as it peeled off my cheek. When I finally looked up, I noticed there were at least six men in the room, all standing around my desk bearing large smiles. They were all staring at me, and after I had made eye contact with a few of them, we all looked around the room at each other, me in confusion, they in delight. Finally, someone spoke.

"You didn't drink that tea, did you?" It was Henry.

"What tea?" I exclaimed.

"Tom left it on the counter in the faculty kitchen by accident. He brought it today to show us. It was his grandmother's. It's been in the family since the First World War. It's over 100 years old."

I looked down at the empty mug, realizing only then that I had fallen asleep on my desk, in the middle of the day, at the university where I taught.

"What's with all of the foliage?" asked one of my colleagues, pointing to a slew of twigs and leaves scattered across my desk and on the floor around my chair. The whole group laughed again and turning to the exit, lumbered slowly out of the office.

THE END

Printed in Great Britain
by Amazon

49279555R00061